CH00798643

BLOOD TRAIL

Across Time

SARAH RUTH SCOTT

authorHOUSE®

AuthorHouse™ UK
1663 Liberty Drive
Bloomington, IN 47403 USA
www.authorhouse.co.uk
Phone: 0800.197.4150

Published by AuthorHouse 05/09/2016

ISBN: 978-1-5246-3399-8 (sc)
ISBN: 978-1-5246-3400-1 (e)

Print information available on the last page.

Any people depicted in stock imagery provided by Thinkstock are models, and such images are being used for illustrative purposes only. Certain stock imagery © Thinkstock.

This book is printed on acid-free paper.

Because of the dynamic nature of the Internet, any web addresses or links contained in this book may have changed since publication and may no longer be valid. The views expressed in this work are solely those of the author and do not necessarily reflect the views of the publisher, and the publisher hereby disclaims any responsibility for them.

ACKNOWLEDGEMENTS

I wish to thank many people for their help and support in making this book possible, first of all my dear family the Sutton's of Ashton Under Lyne in Lancashire for their support and patience. Jeni for reading my work and giving me the heads up, well done to you. To my cover model Kari Ulrichsen for being willing to be photographed as Siena how daring is she. I also thank my loyal readers without you there would be no books and no incentive to continue as a writer. Also thank you to other namely Anja and Ulf from Sweden, Christina Cunningham from South America. As for Daniel Sutton, look out for his name as it will be significant in all future dealings with S.R.S books.

I would also like to say that some of the proceeds or royalties from my books will go to charity, I am concerned with many charities that do so much in our society and all around the world. There are too many to mention but

I refer to cancer research, world aid, child and animal cruelty, places damaged by terrorist attacks such as ground zero (9/11-attack on the twin towers and many other worthy charities.

INTRODUCTION

A woman called Siena enters the future through a picture or time portal and befriends a man Jack who later discovers he is in love with a vampire. However this is just the beginning of his problems as vampire slayers also enter the future and both are faced with more than they bargain for in this fast pace story of romance and intrigue. The story takes the readers through a journey through time meeting interesting characters and danger around every corner. Siena wants to be human again and asks god to help her reach her goal, a guardian angel called Faith appears with a mission to defeat the vampire that cursed her life, in order to be human again she persuades Jack and others to help her achieve this. But the vampires of the future are evil and treacherous, and their body armour protects them from daylight as they travel through time in order to harvest human beings for blood, is there hunger never satisfied as they abduct more and more humans and celebrate their grand feast.

THE BLOOD
TRAIL BEGINS

It was a cold night, the moon was full and the trees blew wildly in the air, in the thick of the forest a woman ran frantically for her life. She had mud on her pale face and torn clothes, she had fear in her green eyes and constantly looked back holding back her hood in order to see her pursuers. She could hear them shouting holding flaming torches and clubs, the loud snapping of twigs suggested they were getting closer. Suddenly she caught her arm on a branch scratching the flesh on her wrist it began to bleed and she fell over another branch down a ditch. Her eyes started to blur as she desperately tried to get to her feet, she noticed a castle in the clearing and began to run towards it. She was followed by two of the men, who began to run behind her, she arrived at the main door, which was open and proceeded down a long corridor. She appeared to know where she was going and entered a room; blood began to trickle down her arm as she gazed at a portrait oil painting of a man. She noticed a strange thing about the painting as the man in the portrait began to look as if he was moving and the background appeared transparent. She put her hand on the picture and her hand seemed to blend into it, so she withdrew her hand in shock, the out of curiosity she placed her hand in a little further. At that moment she heard voices and noticing the blood dripping from her fingers put the rest of her body through the picture. She found herself rushing through some kind of wind tunnel with swirls of light travelling around her pushing her forward leading through another picture. She eventually reached the other end of her journey and landed onto the floor on top of a man.

After wrestling with him, she managed to break free and he stood to his feet and offered a hand to help her to her feet. She slapped his hand and managed to stand by herself looking very annoyed by his actions.

"Get off me and stay away from me" She shouted

"Hey calm down" He replied looking around him "I was only trying to help"

"How did you get on me like that?" She asked

"Well I was admiring that picture" He pointed to the picture "When you jumped out of it and you fell on top of me just to get things in perspective".

"Oh you mean that picture I feel really odd" She said holding her head

"What's wrong?" He said touching her on the arm

"Don't touch me" She said nervously "I warn you I bite"

"I am not going to harm you, I just want to help" He insisted

"So who are you and where the hell am I?" She asked

"I am Jack Clarke and this is an art gallery" Jack said "Don't you know where you are?" He said bewildered by her strange manner.

"I am Siena, I was being chased in a forest and ran into a castle, a weird thing happened, I seemed to enter a picture and landed here. Siena explained

"Wherever here is" She said looking round the room with her green eyes that seemed to sparkle in the light.

"Well you're here now" Jack replied "In the twenty first century"

"What?" Siena was shocked "I am in the future"

"Yes you look as if you have come from medieval times eleventh century maybe, come let's get some air" Jack said leading Siena to the exit

"Seventh century under the reign of King Charles" Siena replied

"The English civil war" Jack said with surprise

"There is a civil war in England?" Siena asked

"I take it hasn't happened yet" Jack thinking he had better not mention that the King was beheaded.

"So this is the future no wonder things seem strange" Siena said looking at the furniture and odd clothes being worn.

Suddenly Siena saw daylight and froze like a statue by the door

"I think I will stay inside for a while" Siena said hesitating and shaking like a leaf.

"Ok let's get a drink in the canteen" Jack suggested

"That sounds good to me" Siena said relieved

They walked towards the canteen passing art displays such as pictures, statues and other strange shaped objects. Siena was bewildered by the displays and appeared disorientated by her surroundings. The clothes that people were wearing also fascinated her; she continued to hold her head sitting at a table.

"So who was chasing you? Jack asked

"Chasing me" Siena thought for a moment "Oh a few strange men with clubs annoyed about something" Siena said not wanting to elaborate and avoiding eye contact.

"Oh that explains a lot" Jack said sarcastically "people can be so touchy"

"Look I have to get back" Siena said worried

"Back where" Jack asked

"Back home of course"

"But you're in danger there" Jack said concerned

"I am not safe here either, I can't explain it but believe me I am" Siena said trembling. "My master would be angry if I don't go back"

"Listen! You don't recognise objects and outside scares you so I can only conclude that you are from the past and that you entered some sort of time portal". Jack said, "I can't think of any other explanation".

"You're speaking nonsense I only know I have to return home" Siena insisted

"Well we need to get back to the picture" Jack explained. "There lies the answer to problems you have been facing".

"You have a master, so does that make you a slave?" Jack said confused

"Sort of we are all slaves and serve one master" Siena tried to explain

"Not me I am a free agent" jack insisted "No one rules me"

They finished their drinks and went back to the area where the picture was being displayed. No one was in the area and the gallery was about to close Siena saw the picture but it didn't seem the same, she went to touch it placing her hand on the canvas but nothing happened. She tried again and suddenly heard shouting from a distance as a guard approached them.

"It seems different somehow" Siena said gazing at it.

"In what way? Jack asked

"It is no longer alive" Siena said tapping it "Just a painting nothing more"

"Don't touch the paintings they are valuable" The guard said

"Sorry" Jack said "I was examining the texture"

"What do I do now?" Siena asked, "I am stuck here in the wrong time".

"I have an idea" Jack said leading her back to the exit.

It was dark outside but it was very busy with a lot of traffic, Jack hailed a taxi and gave the driver his address. When they entered the taxi Siena began to stare at him, she had not really realised how handsome he was with his blue eyes and fair hair, he was clean-shaven and had a prominent chin. He was looking back at her trying to see beyond a dirty face and frowning expression she had removed her hood revealing her long black hair and unusual fringe. She was suddenly startled by a car horn and jumped, then the sound of ambulance sirens, which raced past her window at great speed. She held on to Jacks arm and he could feel the tension in her fingers as they dug into him like a claw.

"Your quite safe Siena believe me" Jack said reassuringly

"I wish I could believe that" Siena said staring out into the streets fascinated by the neon lights, which lit up the area around them.

Jack could feel Siena's heart beating next to him as she drew ever closer to his side, he put his arm around her to reassure her and she began to relax.

They finally reached their destination the taxi stopped outside his apartment, Jack paid the fair and they walked out into the cold dark street. Jack escorted Siena to the apartment block and tried to enter discretely; unfortunately he was stopped by a friend.

Pier was a French friend who had spent a lot of time with Jack during his college days, he was dark skinned and smelt of garlic as Siena was introduced to him she ran into the building. Siena had also noticed a crucifix around his neck, Pier was a catholic and usually wore a rosary. But he had left France with a little Sinicism in mind, his exposure to the wider world made him think that the increased presence of evil was more than enough reason to doubt the existence of any god. The people that professed to be good and such as priests and nuns appeared to have a bad reputation, the exposure of child abuse or forms of fornication turned a lot of people against them. Jack said goodbye to Pier and walked over to a frightened Siena, He never spoke to her but led her into his apartment.

Siena looked around the room then began to yawn and lay on the settee, she soon drifted off to sleep. Jack found a blanket and placed it over her, he then took the phone off the receiver so that she would not be disturbed. He sat close by admiring her beautiful face; he couldn't help feeling that there was more to her than she admitted. He reflected back on his first encounter of her as she jumped out of the picture, from the time portal and falling onto him.

Once she had woken up Jack showed her how to operate the shower, he then left her to wash herself in private, and she couldn't believe the way the shower worked. Letting the water flow down upon her, he had pointed out the shower gel and shampoo and she seemed to be in the shower for a long time. When she came out she was wearing Jacks bathrobe, Jack had washed her clothes and sat watching television. But Siena noticed that he was watching a vampire movie called Van Helsing a vampire slayer. She seemed disturbed by the television alone but worse by the sight of someone killing vampires.

"Oh Siena was everything alright" Jack asked concerned

"Yes I feel a little better now" Siena said smiling "But what is this you are watching"

"Oh I love vampires, but let me turn it off, vampires as if they exist" Jack said turning off the television.

"If you say so" Siena said sitting on the settee "You love vampires seriously?"

"Yes but I know they are not real of course" Jack said confident that he was right.

"Really" Siena said looking into his eyes "Why do you say that?"

"Everybody knows it all began as a story about Dracula" Jack continued

"What if you saw one for yourself, face to face?"

"Well, then I would believe" Jack admitted

Jack dealt with Siena's wounded arm using a bowl of warm water antiseptic and a clean towel.

"This wound needs attention, you really need to go to hospital" Jack advised

"No not that, I will be ok" Siena replied "Really I just to rest"

"But you look pale, you must have lost a lot of blood, you may need a blood transfusion" Jack said concerned "You know they give you blood"

"I said I am alright, its nothing I have had worse" Siena said bluntly "Wait did you say they give you blood?"

"Then let me dress it" Jack said opening a dressing pack "My ex-girlfriend used to be a nurse" Jack explained. "You are definitely not from here are you?"

"I see well I am honestly alright so just dress it please" Siena insisted "And no I am not from here so stop talking about things I don't understand like blood transfusions."

Jack finished cleaning and dressing her arm and then put the remainder of the first aid kit away in the cupboard and returned to sit beside Siena.

"I looked up the seventeenth century on computer and found the castle you were referring to" Jack pointed to the monitor "There it is near the woods"

Meanwhile as they were having their discussion vampires were entering the time portal in search of Siena, they were sent by their master Vermont. He was determined to find Siena and return her to his family.

Siena kept yawning and nodding off to sleep with her legs elevated and her head on the arm of the chair, she looked so fresh and clean, with her hair shining and flowing down with her soft pale skin gleaming. Jack was admiring her as she slept; she had just come into his life and he considered himself very lucky to have her in his home. He was hoping that they would get together as a couple but he was not lucky with women and he had the feeling that she would suddenly disappear probably back through the time portal.

Siena awoke again and looked across at Jack her eyes were glazed and she seemed pale as if she was suffering from anaemia.

"Can I offer you food and a drink?" Jack said concerned

"Yes please" Siena said politely.

Jack went into the kitchen and returned with sandwiches cut and placed neatly on a plate went back out and returned with two mugs of tea with sugar and milk. She put two heaped spoonfuls of sugar in her mug and a tiny drop of milk, she stirred it slowly and took a sip from the mug. They had a brief conversation about Jacks job in a hospital kitchen just around the corner. Then Siena explained about the place she lived in, but seemed to be holding a lot of information back particularly about her family. Jack had not noticed, but Siena had no reflection in the mirror, that evening Pier visited Jack but Siena avoided him acting quite rudely. But Siena was trying to protect herself and avoid the crucifix that he wore around his neck, anything that would harm or destroy her, or even expose her as a vampire.

That night Jack offered to sleep on the settee while Siena slept on the bed, Siena reluctantly accepted. That night the moon was full and the sky was clear and full of stars Siena looked out through the window watching the wind blowing the trees. Siena opened the window and then crept towards the door and watched Jack sleeping, she then returned to the window and jumped out onto a tree and down to the street. She came to an alley where a woman was walking alone, suddenly she was joined by two men as they got closer one of them grabbed her the other man then spoke to her.

"Now just do as we say and you wont get hurt" He said in a deep gravely voice

She began to struggle and scream so one of the men slapped her knocking her to the ground. The other began to pull down his trousers while the other man held her; she continued to struggle as he attempted to remove her clothes.

Siena raced forward and knocked the man over with his trousers down his ankles, she had changed into a vampire and seemed to have incredible strength. She hit the other man and knocked him into a wall, he fell down the brickwork with his head bleeding.

"Go run away" Siena said but the woman didn't need telling she ran from the alley with great speed.

Siena walked back to the man who was conscious and pulling up his trousers, she grabbed him and held him tightly. Her eyes began stare at him, putting him into a trance.

"Let's make love" Siena said smiling

"Wow ok" He replied excitedly

Siena kissed his neck and then pierced his skin with her fangs and began sucking the blood from his body until he was drain of life and his limp body fell to the ground. She wiped her bloody mouth and then walked over to the unconscious man and did the same to him, sucked his blood and left him dead in the alley.

Siena had begun to feel better and wandered back to the apartment entering it via the window as she did earlier. She got undressed and settled into bed feeling that she could rest comfortably knowing that she had received her life sustenance, human blood.

The next morning Siena was fast asleep and Jack was in the shower, he had switched on the television and the news was on. The two bodies discovered in the alley were the main feature, but also Pier had been murdered in the same way.

The question was did Siena murder Pier because he too had two puncture marks in his neck, in the same way that Siena had killed the two men. The news report repeated throughout the day, Jack saw it later as he returned from work later that day. He avoided disturbing Siena knowing that she needed the rest.

He looked in on her sleeping soundly, lying across the bed with her head facing away from the window. He opened the curtains and Siena's back reacted to the sunlight by burning slightly.

"Please shut the curtains my body is sensitive to light, I have some kind of illness that reacts to light" Siena explained

"You never told me" Jack said concerned

Jack offered her a drink in a clear glass, a sort of strawberry cordial drink which she looked at and turned her head away.

"Please take that away from me" She shouted and began waving her hands in the air.

It reminded Siena of blood that she was once given in a goblet by Count Vermont as a form of ritual when she joined the family of vampire.

Siena sat beside Jack listening to him as he discussed the murders; she had tried to show no emotion as he went into graphic detail. She wanted to forget the experience and knew that she would venture out for yet another night, seeking out victims in order to obtain their blood and live another day.

Jack noticed that she seemed disturbed and sat closer to her, she glanced at him and smiled leaning on his arm and resting her head on his shoulder.

"You are very kind to me and a real gentleman" Siena said smiling

"I know how to respect women and as you have come from another time you are naturally bewildered by what you see and hear". Jack explained

"But you can teach me and show me your world" Siena said looking into his eyes

"Yes I can but so much has changed since your time, cars, planes and telephones" Jack said trying to imagine what she was thinking.

"Inventions and scary machines that are so noisy" Siena had not taken her eyes off Jack, she began to feel a tingle down her spine and the hair stood up at the back of her neck.

Jack drew ever closer to her, looking into her green eyes and feeling strange in her presence. It was like something he had never felt before and began to relax he began to drift off to sleep. At this point Siena began to kiss him on the lips and his neck, then she suddenly changed and her fangs appeared. She leapt off the settee and onto the floor, she had realised what she had done by hypnotising Jack and trying to bite his neck, fortunately she managed to stop herself in time.

Jack awoke from his trance and saw Siena sat on the floor; she had a suspicious look on her face and appeared nervous.

"What has just happened to me?" Jack asked her

"I think you fainted" Siena said in response "You were sat with me and made me jump when you suddenly woke up" Siena hoped that he was convinced by her explanation.

Jack seemed to accept her explanation and never mentioned the situation again. Siena was more aware of her actions after this time and the next time they were close was not due to her but Jack who made advances to her. Jack had been going out to work during the day and with Siena at night, Siena continued to sneak out and find her own blood bank choosing people who were in her eyes wicked or deviant souls. This was her justification for taking draining their blood and ending their life the only way a vampire knows feeding off humans and surviving leaving a blood trail.

Jack cuddled up to Siena and put his arm around her, Siena felt uneasy, as she was afraid of what she might do to him. Jack began to kiss her on the lips and she felt her heart begin to beat faster, her desire for him was become too great to resist and she kissed him back. A rush of passion overcome them both and they were soon in the throws of making love, items of clothing were removed they were both wild as they seemed to tear at each others clothes until they were naked. They headed for the bedroom and continued making love, neither relented as they went from the bedroom into the shower. Their naked flesh became entwined as the water from the shower trickled gently down their body and the steam from the water misted the glass cubical.

The months passed by and they lived the same way with Jack working at the hospital and coming home to a special lady and Siena at home cleaning the apartment and cooking delicious meals. Life seemed perfect for a while, but Siena continued to sleep part of the day and went out at night for her usual feast. Jack explained about Pier's death to Siena.

Pierre was walking past the forest when he heard a female voice coming from the trees, he followed the voice into the thick of the forest. When he stopped he was met by a woman who he couldn't see properly, she managed to hypnotise him before attacking him sinking her fangs into his neck and draining the blood from him. It must have been like being attacked by a savage animal.

But the vampire had to survive and the blood was keeping her alive, however what Siena failed to realise was that she was not alone, the time portal had invited others through and Tom the vampire slayer had followed her through the time portal along with others namely vampires.

Siena walked through the woods, she reached a stream and crossed an old wooden bridge that she recognised from her past. She looked down into the stream and saw her mother's face in the water as if she was really there.

"Mother help me, show me the way I am so lost, I have met a man called Jack and I want to live with him forever, I don't want to live alone as a vampire, living off other humans".

"My child I died here as you know, killed by slayers, you must choose your own course I miss you too", She said "You have to either stay here or return home to your own time, only you can choose what direction to take." With those words she faded away.

"Mother don't go please" Siena pleaded put her mother was gone.

INTO THE DARKNESS

Yet again it was a full moon Siena laid beside Jack she was feeling particularly weak and looked very pale, she looked at Jacks naked neck and suddenly her fangs appeared and her eyes became wild staring at her victims flesh. As she approached him slowly and breathed cold air on his neck, he suddenly awoke and turned his head towards her. Then looked in horror as she was still trying to bite his neck and suck his blood.

"Oh my god!" Jack shouted, "You're a vampire, you are actually a vampire, I have been sleeping with a vampire"

Jack pushed her away and she fell off the bed, she tried to get up but Jack pointed to her angrily and she stayed on the floor.

"I have been sleeping with a vampire, its all coming clear to me now, Pier had eaten garlic and he had a crucifix, so you avoided him, tell me did you kill him?"

"No I didn't" Siena said starting to change back to human form. "But then other vampires could have travelled through the picture as I did"

"You mean the time portal, so there are more like you?" Jack said worried

"And what about that vampire movie, you knew you were a vampire when we were watching it and said nothing" Jack began shaking his head "You were going to bite me and drain me of my blood".

"I know I'm sorry" Siena said with her head bowed "I wanted you to be like me and live forever".

"Well you might have warned me"

"It's not exactly what you bring into a conversation" Siena said upset "Oh by the way I am a vampire"

"Oh I see you're sorry that helps until I sleep again and you actually bite me". Jack said upset.

"For god sake I didn't plan to be a vampire, I didn't wake one morning and say I want to be a vampire or seek Count Vermont and say make me a vampire" Siena said angrily. "It's a curse not a pleasure"

"So how did it happen?" Jack asked

"I was walking in the woods one night when I heard the breaking of branches I ran further in to the wood and came out in a clearing. I began to run and was suddenly surrounded by bats that turned into vampires; two of them grabbed me and took me to the castle Vermont where I met the Count. He put me in some kind of trance and then bit my neck draining my blood, then he did a very odd thing he sent blood back into my body which brought me back from death making me a vampire. I then had to rely on him to keep me alive showing me how to take blood and survive in my present state" Siena explained.

"But it all began long before that night, for as a child my sister Catherine and I would go to bed and our father used to tell us stories about vampires, witches and werewolves. He was so knowledgeable about goblins and other creatures and told convincing tales of many things as if he had experienced them himself. We would sit in our candle lit bedroom watching the flickering of the light and observing the hot wax melting gently like tear drops down the candle. We imagined the creatures that my father mimicked so well, the sound of an owl hooting or the cry of a wolf. He told of vampire slayers like John Stokes, the best slayer of his time who would hunt down vampires and werewolves alike, killing them with stakes or silver bullets according to their kind. Pity the day that those devilish creatures ventured through the forest, when Stokes was around, leading his huntsmen searching in the darkness for their prey. Hunting witches was a common thing of our day any poor old hag was marked for trial and execution, tortured and kept awake in order to confess their sins and admit to their divination. Sorcery and magic would be committed though never truly proven and yet some poor wretch had to die, no one who was accused was ever set free. My father used to go out at night, while my mother stayed at home sitting by an open fire and resting in a rocking chair. I would pretend to be asleep and then as I got older I would venture out through the window and follow my father. It was at this time that I discovered his secret, for he was none other than the said John Stokes they spoke of assuming the name in order to strike fear into those he planned to slay. He spoke to his group and advised that they should stay close and not venture off alone, he warned of the dangers of trying to tackle the enemy alone. Strong are their powers and swift to take you off and kill you or worse make you one of their own, an undead creature or a person who is neither dead nor alive, living in perpetual darkness. Here you stand with just the light of the full moon to guide you, with the blood of man keeping you alive. Woe be you if you live this way amongst the demons and cursed for all time. When I was out following one night that's when I was grabbed but I had been seeing a man in the forest who I considered gentle and kind. His name was Matthew a farmer from a neighbouring village, a hard working young man so quiet and shy. He was waiting for me in the forest one night when he was taken by two female vampires called Emma and Lara they teased him because he was shy before feasting on his blood. Then another female vampire called Miranda made him her own by giving of her blood in his neck, he was a vampire and a slave to Count Vermont. When I became a vampire I journeyed with him in the woods, my father appeared and was shocked to see that I had changed; he disowned me and lifted his bow to kill me. Matthew noticed what was happening and jumped in front of me, he was killed by the missile that was shot from the bow and immediately disintegrated. I escaped on this occasion I ran and ran until I reached the castle and found the picture, or as you call it the time portal, I entered it and met you.

"That's quite a story" Jack said astonished

"You don't believe me?" Siena said sadly

"Yes I do but I must confess it's a lot to take in and we need to get help for you" Jack said concerned

"Who is going to help a blood sucking vampire?" Siena said

"Have you tried asking God?" Jack said confident that he had the answer to her dilemma.

"God? He helps good people not people like me" Siena became tearful

"Why don't you go to church and ask him, he is merciful and kind" Jack said trying to reason with her.

"If I enter the house of god I will die, I cannot even enter the doorway" Siena said becoming agitated

"Stop! My theory is this, if you are to be helped then you will be protected God will see the sincerity in your heart and help you". Jack felt that his explanation was enough to convince her to enter the church.

"Well what have I got to lose, I could risk being destroyed in church or by Tom the vampire slayer" Siena thought for a moment "Alright I will do it".

That evening Siena entered the graveyard and began walking up the pathway towards the church, suddenly she was startled by the voice of a woman.

"Are you going somewhere Siena?" Miranda's voice was heard clearly by Siena

Siena turned around and saw a blonde haired woman floating above her head, when she turned back two other women with darker hair stood in front of her. "We have been searching for you" Lara said with a hiss.

"Yes you have been hiding from us" Emma said floating in front of her.

"I stumbled into this picture and found myself here" Siena said trying to get past them "I never wanted to be here"

"My dear you must come with us to the master" Miranda said blocking her way.

"Yes the master is angry with you, you have disappointed him" Lara said also blocking her way.

"Come let's go" Miranda insisted

During the scuffle an arrow was fired into the air and hit the Miranda in the chest, she immediately disintegrated this was followed by another arrow that narrowly missed Emma. Siena ducked behind a gravestone and Lara flew away from Siena narrowly dodging arrows.

Siena entered the church aware that Tom the slayer was watching her from a distance, but she was hoping that he wouldn't follow her. He seemed surprised that she was entering a church and stopped by a tree waiting for her to reappear. But Siena walked towards the alter and tried to look at the cross in front of her, she gazed into the eyes of the statue of Mary holding Jesus in her arms. Tears filled her eyes and she fell to her knees, she then sobbed for a while then began speaking in a low voice.

"God please help me I know that I have done bad things and even caused deaths, I am cursed as a vampire and want to be human again" Siena paused and looked through the gaps in her fingers "I haven't disintegrated so I presume that you have heard my prayer and considering it".

At that moment she heard a voice coming from behind her

"Siena" came a soft female voice "Don't be afraid"

Siena turned to see an image appear it was an angel wearing a white dress and carrying a key, which was tied to a sash and hung down from her neck to her thigh.

"I am Faith, I am a guardian angel and have a message from God" Faith said sincerely.

"An angel but why are you here are you going to kill me?" Siena said concerned

"No I am here to help you, God is merciful and wants to help you, if you are prepared to help yourself, are you willing to do this and put your faith in god?" Faith asked.

"Yes of course, so what do I do?" Siena said eagerly

"Then you must perform a number of tasks to prove yourself worthy" Faith continued "You need to go back in time to where you became a vampire, you then need to collect a series of objects and take them to the castle Vermont the final object is worn by Count Vermont himself and this is a pendant to take this from him he must die and you will rid the land of evil". Faith said

"So about these other objects where do I find them?" Siena asked

"One will lead to another and each one will introduce you to someone who needs help and you will provide that help as part of your task". Faith explained.

"But what about me wont I need help in order to aid others?" Siena asked

"You must promise not to take blood from others and not kill anyone but the evil ones, you will be helped but you must have Faith in God". Faith said touching her wrist

"But I am a vampire I take blood because I would die without it" Siena said concerned.

"Look at your wrist Siena" Faith said pointing to a shining bracelet

"What's this" Siena asked

"This will prevent you from taking blood and keep you alive, never remove it this will protect you" Faith explained "Try to divert your mind from evil thoughts look only to good things and what is right".

"Thank you" then thought for a moment "Can Jack come with me?" Siena asked

"It has already been arranged my friend Harmony has visited him" Faith said "May God bless you and have a safe journey" With those words Faith vanished.

At that moment Tom the slayer entered the church and ran towards her, he knocked her to the ground and pulled a stake from his bag. Siena held her arm up in order to protect her and the glow from the bracelet shone into Toms eyes, he yelled out and dropped the stake and scrambled to find it.

At that moment Jack entered the church, he ran up to Tom and disarmed him.

"Siena I was visited by an angel called Harmony and she told me what I need to do in order to help you. She told me everything about you becoming human and what is required, I am coming with you, I want to help you"

"You have helped me Jack" Siena insisted

"I know but I don't want to lose you" Jack said holding her "I want to help you defeat the evil ones.

"Come with me because I feel the same, I want you close by my side" Siena said

"Tom we need your help in order to find Count Vermont, are you with us?" jack asked

"Tom help me become human again lets destroy the evil that has cursed our people" Siena said pleading with him

"I am with you what do we do?" Tom asked

"Go to the gallery and enter the time portal" Jack suggested

"Exactly we must return home Tom" Siena said.

"I am ready to face the evil of the dark world" Tom said positively

The three arrived at the gallery hoping to find the time portal; they searched for the picture that Jack would recognise, to his delight the portrait of a lady appeared. But it seemed just like the other paintings stunning and attractive, with nothing special to tell them that this was a time portal. It had no depth and looked nothing like the painting that

Siena had came from and fell on Jack. Desperately they waited for the picture to change; meanwhile the security guards were ushering people out of the gallery. One guard approached them looking very official and determined to close the gallery on time.

"We are about to close" He said in a stern manner

"Can I ask you something about this painting?" Jack said diverting him away from the others.

"Yes of course it was imported from Germany, it was originally the property of Count Vermont said to have been a vampire" The security officer said pleased to provide Jack with the information "The painting is said to be enchanted and holds many secrets, obviously this is ridiculous just like the legend of vampires"

"Of course" Jack replied watching Siena and Tom vanish into the picture behind the guard.

Siena landed in the same room where she began her journey through time, she looked at the portrait watching Tom appear. It seemed a long time before Jack arrived, he fell to the ground and seemed dazed lying on the floor, both Siena and Tom helped him up.

"Welcome to Crompton castle" Siena said

"So this is it, the castle where you came from" Jack said holding his head

"Are you alright?" Tom asked

"Yes I had to lose the guard before following you, he took some losing believe me". Jack said looking back at the picture.

"I think we ought to go before anyone sees us" Tom said opening the door and stepping into the corridor.

They walked outside looking for the right direction to find the giant Fargo who would help them find Laura the witch.

Fargo was not difficult to find sitting on a rock, he was an eight-foot man with a brown beard, muscular body with long hair tied back in a pony tail. He had a fat broken nose and a scar on his chin; he appeared to have been involved in battle previously.

They approached Fargo confident that he would greet them with open arms and willingly help them. But the giant seemed hostile and defensive and resented Siena being there and wanting his help, he didn't trust her suspecting that she might lead them into a trap when they arrived at Castle Vermont if not before.

"You must be Fargo" Siena said offering to shake his hand

"I am" Said Fargo refusing to shake her hand "I have something for you"

"A red stone, perhaps a ruby" Siena said realising that he didn't trust her.

"Yes a ruby representing the blood of Vermont" Fargo said looking at the other two men. "It also represents the blood spilt on this land.

"Oh yes this is Jack and Tom they are helping us" Siena said

"We travel tomorrow you can stay in my cave behind those trees" Fargo said

"It is surrounded by garlic to ward away the vampires" Fargo looked at Siena and back at the trees covering the cave "But how will you enter the cave?"

"I have a protective bracelet which is helping me to survive at present" Siena explained, "Providing I do well I will be protected"

"Then its up to you to avoid evil and follow to path to goodness" Fargo said sincerely.

"Yes I must, I know this" Siena said

They entered the cave and Fargo found an area for them to sleep, the cave was well lit with burning torches every few yards. The walls were decorated with paintings of birds and wild animals; a book lay on a table near by written on the cover were the words 'best poems'. The floor seemed gritty and elements of sand were present indicating the presence of the coast, like a sandy beach.

"Are you hungry?" Fargo asked

"A little" Jack admitted

"Then lets feast my friends" Fargo said uncovering food on a table

Siena didn't eat much and became very pale and looking very tired

"I think I will just rest if you don't mind" Siena said walking towards the bedded area.

Fargo watched her leave the area and looked at the others in disbelief

"I don't trust her, she may be protected but she's still a vampire" Fargo said

"She is ok, I have been with her for a while and I was safe" Jack said looking at them both.

They spoke for a while then settled to bed, but during the night Siena was approached and the person concerned had a stake in his hand. He pressed it against her chest and attempted to hammer it into her chest with a wooden mallet. Suddenly Jack jumped in the way and got injured from the stake that pieced him in his side.

"Fargo stop it now!" Tom shouted, "Trust us she is of no danger to you"

"You maniac you nearly killed her" Jack said with his side bleeding

Siena hugged him then saw the blood "Help him Tom please"

Siena then turned to Fargo and spoke to him "Fargo let me tell you something, I have come here to defeat evil, to change my life and with the will of God become human again" Siena said angrily "Destroy me and you will continue to see people die.

"I will not try to harm you again, I promise" Fargo said ashamed of himself

"I want to be your friend and for us all to work together and destroy Vermont and his vampires" Siena said putting her hand out in friendship.

Fargo shuck her by the hand "I am sorry" He said sincerely.

"It's alright now lets help Jack" Siena said going back to Jack

"He is fine the stake just caught the skin" Tom explained

They all rested and the next morning Tom asked for weapons to protect themselves from Count Vermont's followers, Fargo showed them weapons crossbows with deadly arrows powerful enough to kill the enemy.

"Crossbows and other weapons" Fargo said

"A complete arsenal for us all" Tom said happily

"Well don't miss and hit me" Siena said jokingly

"I will watch out for you Siena after all you have to kill Count Vermont" Tom said discussed and disappointed with Fargo.

They went in search of Laura the white witch; Fargo knew exactly where to find her and seemed happy to lead the way.

LAURA THE WITCH

They saw the cave amongst the trees and bushes; they followed a small path towards it. Once inside they were taken by surprise as they saw all kinds of treasures collected from various places that Laura had visited. A picture of Laura was hung on the wall for all to see, that is the people she would normally invite to eat with her. Laura was a beautiful woman with gold blonde hair, pointed ears and glowing white teeth. She had a pale complexion and light blue eyes, to say she was a witch she was not the type that Jack had read about from books. He imagined an old hag stirring a caldron of dead bats and toads, possibly a broomstick and dolls that would simulate someone she despised with pins stuck in their bodies in order to harm them.

"This is no witches place" Jack said almost disappointed

"Not all witches are dark and sinister, some are good witches" Siena said

"I have never heard of a good witch" Jack said confused

"Perhaps we should go" Fargo said concerned

At that moment Laura appeared with her golden hair and a long pastel green coloured dress, she had blue eyes and her long hair was platted and styled, she had pointed ears and it looked as if she had a tiara on her head. She seemed to swoop down to them from above and was displeased at their presence.

"Who are you and why have you entered my home uninvited? Laura asked

"I am Siena I have been sent to you from the future a guardian angel Faith sent me to you" Siena explained.

"Then you are the one who is going to rid this world of evil?" Laura asked.

"Yes I guess I am" Siena said confidently "And you are Laura the witch that will help me".

"I have something for you" Laura looked in a treasure chest and produced a bracelet for her other wrist, which she put on her and kissed it.

"This will protect you from the vampires and from evil" Laura said "But never remove it until the evil has been destroyed".

"Are you not going to travel with us?" Siena asked

"No but I will be observing you and with you in spirit" Laura said

"So, which way do we go now?" Jack asked

"The home of Lily the child" Tom said

"Yes she is just over that hill my dear" Laura said pointing outside the cave.

"Thank you Laura" Siena said

"Please stay for tea, share my table" Laura said making a table appear.

On the table was an array of fine food and drinks, it was like a royal banquet fit for a King or Queen. A roast chicken stood freshly cooked in the centre of the table, garnished with sauce and surrounded by roast potatoes. This was accompanied by a selection of cooked vegetables and other savoury delights.

Help yourself to what you desire my friends and please leave nothing to spoil, for all is edible and will fill you for your journey. Siena noticed the goblets of berry juice and her mind drifted back to Vermont's blood ceremony, she visualised the other vampires drinking blood and killing some of their victims.

Everyone ate the food and drank the various juices that were on offer, nothing was wasted but a few heads began to droop as they were tired after their journey to Laura's cave. So they rested and Laura watched over them so that all could sleep through the night.

The next day each of them prepared for their long journey ahead, Laura was resting while they all washed and ate breakfast. Laura had a nice area for them to wash in private further inside the cave, but in safe proximity in case of trouble. By the time Laura awoke they were all ready to go, Tom was the first to get ready and stood waiting for the others.

"Good luck I hope you do well" Laura said smiling

Siena couldn't help admitting that she was disappointed that Laura would not be with them, if for nothing else she could have provided her with moral support and female companionship. But Laura had her own reasons not to join them and was reluctant to share them with Siena or her friends.

So Siena and her companions continued on their arduous journey travelling over the hillside in search of Lily. Lily was running around a garden beside an old cottage, she was a small nine year old girl with ginger wavy hair with pointed ears and blue eyes; she had a round face and wore a yellow patterned dress. She saw Siena and smiled sweetly standing still near a tree, she had a lovely smile, and her ginger hair was blowing about in the wind

"She too had pointed ears like a pixie" Jack commented "This is like a fairy tale"

"Hello she said sweetly I am Lily" She said politely "She said giggling at Jack's remark"

"I am Siena" Siena replied, "This is Jack, Tom and Fargo"

"I have something for you Siena" Lily said running into the house

"Pixie ears, really Jack" Siena remarked "That is so normal here"

Lily returned with a ring

"This belonged to my mother who was killed by vampires a while ago, you must put it on your finger" Lily explained "It will guide you to the castle Vermont"

"Thank you Lily are you joining us?" Siena asked

"No she cant it's too dangerous" Tom said

"I am coming, please Siena I won't be any trouble and I can help cook for you" Lily said.

"I want her with me" Siena insisted "She will be safe with us".

"Well you will have to protect her yourself" Tom said

"I don't mind get your things together Lily" Siena said "I will come in the house with you" Siena said holding her hand and leading her inside.

Inside the cottage the furniture was mostly made of wood and at back of the cottage was a small but quaint kitchen. Lily led Siena up the stairs she took her into a small room and packed a small rucksack with some of her clothes. Then she took a small cuddly bear and stuffed it in as deep as she could so that only the head was showing.

"I am ready" Lily said smiling and placing a small book in her bag

"Listen Lily it is going to be dangerous, I wouldn't like anything to happen to you, and don't you have any family?" Siena asked concerned

"No one at all I have had to live alone" Lily said "My book keeps me company"

"Very well let's go Lily" Siena said leading the way down the stairs and outside to join the others.

They walked across a bridge entering a forest, Siena was curious to know what was written in the book that fascinated Lily but she never asked.

They camped in the forest overnight Lily began to sing like a nightingale, her voice was soft and melodically they all listened to her intently as she sang of happy times. They all had supper and discussed their journey. Then Lily began to read her book out loud

"The poet writes his final line about things that couldn't be; he lives his life in solitude with things you cannot see. Hidden away in a fortress tower so high upon a hill, lost within his solitude with dreams he could not fulfil". Lily paused to observe her audience reaction then continued. "A trapped talent within a cell within his mind fresh thoughts do dwell, a man that is trapped within his mind, here the lost poet may dwell. Always thinking about the people you create, when your asleep fresh thoughts you motivate. Like a person within a person or fictitious people within a dream and nightmares make you awake and no one will here you scream".

"That's really intense" Jack said looking at the others "Deep and meaningful"

"Is that from your own mind?" Siena asked

"It came to me" Lily said turning the page "May I read on?"

"Of course" Fargo said smiling "Tell us more".

"So daylight is over and darkness will end the day, the candles burn so low and you must lose your way, and just as the hot sun melts the snow you must leave this life and go" she recited the poem then sang the final part. "The poet write his final line about things that could not be, the poet write his final line for me".

They all clapped and then all kissed and hugged her; everyone was impressed but thought it was just a poem and not a real event.

"I wonder how such a wonderful poem and song came to you" Siena said hugging her.

Soon after the discourse about the poetry they went to sleep, all but Tom who took the first watch sitting on the ground with his crossbow firmly in his hand

Meanwhile at Vermont's castle the vampires were preparing to do battle with anyone who was protecting Siena, each of the vampires were eager to avenge their own kind and blamed Siena for abandoning them. But they wanted Siena alive to face Count Vermont and humble herself to her master, to seek forgiveness and be his bride.

"You flock, you servants of evil" Vermont shouted "To you feel my anger, my pain, and my hunger, one of my children has betrayed me" He raised his arms

"Master we are with you" One male vampire said kneeling at his feet.

"Serpious fetch me my cloak" He said looking down on the limp creature disfigured by illness

"Yes master" Serpious groined

"Master let me go after Siena and bring her back" Another vampire said as she also sat beneath Vermont.

"My dear Alicia I know you want to avenge your sister Miranda but there is time and you are precious to me" He said putting his hand on her head. "I want Martha and

Verity to capture the little girl Lily and then Siena is sure to come".

"I will send Stuart and Serpious to lead my army into attack after midnight and we will have two armies one to divert fire on my people and the other to take the girl. Siena will regret her actions, Lara you have done well to inform me of her plans to destroy me.

It was midnight and the moon was full, the forest was quiet until the first attack took place as a swarm of vampire bats flew over them, followed by flying vampires. It threw everyone into confusion as they watched the bats descend; this was followed by a second attack that was even more intense. Lily was suddenly lifted off the ground by one of the vampires; Tom took aim but was stopped by Fargo.

"Stop! You could hit Lily" Fargo shouted

"But they have taken her" Tom shouted back

"They won't harm her, they want me" Siena said "She is their bargaining tool".

"You promised to keep her safe" Fargo shouted "I might have known a vampire couldn't keep her word".

"Silence Fargo we all let Lily down after all we all said we would protect her" Tom said.

The group were confused after Lily had gone and they were determined to carry on and seek the lost poet in the fortress close by. Lily had dropped her book when she was captured, so at least they could find the lost poet easily.

Fargo had his reason for hating vampires as his wife and two children were killed by vampires, they died horrible deaths and their bodies left in the woods. Fargo threatened to avenge them by killing every vampire who walked the earth, or terrorised the land and satisfied their thirst for blood. Lily had left a clue behind, her book was lying on the ground for all to see.

"Of course that's it" Tom said

"What's wrong Tom?" Siena asked

"The lost poet, I know where he is" Tom said

"So do I" Fargo said pointing to a forest

"Through the forest and hidden away in a fortress tower high upon a hill" Tom said confidently.

"Here the lost poet may dwell" Siena finished his sentence.

"We need to go into the forest" Fargo said.

THE LOST POET

They noticed a fortress tower high upon a hill this is where the lost poet was said to dwell according to the poem. As they approached the tower they noticed a small door as they entered it they noticed stone steps that seemed to spiral to the top of the tower. They all went up the steps and arrived at another door, Tom pushed the door open and discovered a large room with a desk, a small table and a bed. On the table were candle sticks, a thick book and a coat hanging at the back of a chair. On the desk were other candlesticks, an open book a quill and ink well. The bed had a cover over it with an interesting pattern on it; in the centre was an embroidered crest.

Suddenly to their astonishment a figure appeared near the desk, it was a man dressed in old medieval clothes; he had long white hair and looked about sixty. He looked directly at Siena and spoke to her in a gentle voice.

"Who do you seek?" He asked

"We seek the lost poet" Siena replied

"Why do you seek him?" He said suspiciously

"He has something for me, I am on a quest to kill count Vermont" Siena said bravely.

"I am the lost poet, my name is John Gilbert Green and this is my home" Green said proudly.

"You live here in the tower?" Siena said looking round

"Yes this is my humble home and here is where I write my poems" Green pointed to his parchment on the desk "I need a quiet place to create my work"

"I just need a quill and I will be on my way, for we have a child to find captured by the Count". Siena said sadly

"I am sorry to here that I am but an image before you and my soul is also captured, I can only say follow your journey to your destination and you will find your child and me" Green said smiling "I sent a message to her it's in the book that you hold in your hand".

With those words he vanished and the quill was in front of her to take to Count Vermont's castle. The lost poet's voice could be still heard even after he had vanished, he was drawing the party to the castle in order to be found and set free. Siena led the partly out of the tower and back into the forest and towards another castle near by where King Robert lived, he was a King without a kingdom.

A KING WITHOUT
A KINGDOM

The man sat on the king's throne he seemed sad and lost wearing a hat and no crown, he was of royal by blood but Count Vermont had invaded his kingdom with his vampires. The castle and the village was invaded and the people were either murdered with their bodies drained of blood, some fled to the caves or other places of safety, some were turned into vampires and increased Count Vermont's ever growing army.

Siena and her friend walked towards the castle, small green man appeared holding a long spear. He had long black hair and a fat nose; he had a thick belt around his large waist and spoke with a high voice.

"Who goes there? He said pointing his spear towards them.

"Its Siena and friends, we have come to see the King" Siena said positively.

"You're Siena, the vampire?" He asked

"Yes that's me" Siena said "But I am no longer known as a vampire".

"Siena I know all about you and Laura the witch" He said lowering his spear.

"You know Laura?" Siena asked "Your name means special inspirational empathetic natural beauty and with attributes to many to mention"

"And I am Bramble and yes she is known throughout the kingdom". Bramble said smiling at Siena in a creepy kind of way.

Bramble led them to the King who remained sat on the throne, He sat stroking his beard the party walked towards him and bowed.

"Tut tut, don't bow before me I am no king, see I have no kingdom" He swept his arms in each direction "See no one but us".

"But you are still a King" Siena said

"My kingdom was taken from me" The king stood up and shouted in temper "I am not a king and my kingdom has been scattered in the wind, I have been left to care for myself and the Count lives in luxury with my servants and subjects.

So come and laugh at the man who once was a king, I am now but a grain of sand on the beach or desert". King Robert said bitterly.

"Then let us find Count Vermont and destroy his evil only then can we restore your throne and kingdom to what it was" Siena said.

"Yes your highness I am Tom the slayer and I have served you before as blacksmith, Fargo was one of your guards so we have served you and will serve you again I promise". Tom said encouragingly.

"So how did you find me?" The king asked

"Through an angel called Faith and a witch called Laura" Siena explained

"I once condemned Laura as I did the vampires" King Robert said shying.

"And yet you have statues of vampires all the way down the corridors of this castle" Tom said confused.

"What are you talking about I have no statues of vampires" King Robert said frowning.

At that moment the so called statues began to break away from the walls and flying towards the great hall, each detached themselves from the wall assisted by wicked green goblin Bramble who had obviously tricked and ambushed them. They all reached the hall and surrounded Siena and her friends.

"We have come for Siena, you must all surrender or die" One of the vampires said.

"Yes we want only Siena, kill the others" She hissed showing her fangs.

Bramble waved his spear about and tried to look menacing, but he just appeared silly in front of his vampire friends.

At that moment Laura appeared and immediately cast a spell on him leaving him in a giant bubble, He was kicking, yelling and trying to break free. As he was their mascot, his capture confused the vampires for a moment. They looked at each other for inspiration and then attacked everyone in sight. Laura stunned each one with her wand while Tom and Siena destroyed them with their crossbows, firing deadly arrows into their hearts. Each one dispersed into dust and disappeared the battle went on for half an hour until all the vampires were destroyed.

"Thank god that's over" Jack said sighing with relief.

"When are we going to be finally free from them vampires" Tom said lowering his crossbow.

"When we destroy Count Vermont" Siena said sweeping back her hair.

"We should rest here tonight" Tom advised.

"Siena are you alright?" Jack asked

"Yes apart from that strange little man" Siena looked at Bramble

"He is of no importance" Tom said

Bramble was removed from the bubble bound with rope and led to the Counts castle; King Robert made peace with Laura and promised that when his kingdom was restored she would become his personal adviser.

Siena and her friends continued their quest, mindful of their mission to free the villagers and kill the enemy, removing the evil from the land. On their journey Fargo was attacked by blood sucking bats while on watch it was his biggest dread and he was saved by Siena and Tom who managed to fight them off. Later on their journey Siena had a snake wrapped around her neck which Fargo destroyed and threw it into a bush. Jacks fear were heights, walking over bridges made him nervous looking down into rivers or rocky areas beneath him, they crossed many to reach the castle. As for Siena she was afraid of the full moon and although she wore the bracelets she was still affected by the desire for blood, she was looking forward to being human again.

"Siena I truly love you" Jack said sincerely

"I love you too" Siena replied kissing Jack on the lips.

"But I fear myself and my desires" Siena looked down

"I don't understand" Jack replied.

"My thirst for blood, sometimes it is hard to fight and being near you makes it worse" Siena sighed and stood to her feet. "Will this nightmare ever end".

"Be patient you are doing well" Jack advised her "Trust in god"

"Faith told me it would be difficult" Siena said looking into Jacks eyes.

"You will get there, reach your goal and we will be together" Jack explained holding her firmly by the arms.

Laura approached them with her long blonde hair flowing and her dress sparkling under the moonlight.

"It's a beautiful night" Laura said

"Yes it is but the moon is full" Siena said pointing upwards

"Be brave Siena and think of the future" Laura said smiling

"I wanted Jack and I to live forever" Siena said

"Who wants to live forever" Laura said looking up at the moon "Not me"

"Not me" Jack said looking into Siena's eyes "definitely not me", Jack then looked across at the moon.

"I desire only one thing, a happy kingdom" Laura said touching them both on the arm "And of course your happiness" Laura smiled and walked away.

THE EVIL OF COUNT VERMONT

After a long hazardous journey through a rough tureen with swamps, reptiles and other dangers, Siena and her friends reached Count Vermont's castle.

From the moment they arrived they could sensed the danger and smelt rotting flesh of human and animal carcasses. Dried blood stains could be clearly seen on the filthy walls and floors, along with dust and cobwebs. The corridors were dimly lit and Tom advised them to use lighted wooden faggots as torches as they moved closer to the hall way.

Eventually they arrived in a large open area with an enormous stairway leading to the upper level with rooms running off in all directions. Suddenly the count stood surrounded by his evil army of vampires they were all assembled ready to attack each of them eager to take the blood from the humans. Laura headed off to find Lily and whoever else they had captured; she went straight towards the dungeons undetected making herself in visible. She used her wand to disarm the guards causing them to collapse in a heap on the floor. Then took the keys from his belt and unlocked the large door to the dungeon, finding many people inside including Lily. However there was no sign of John Gilbert Green better known as the lost poet or his work, Lily said that she had searched for him in the dungeons but to no avail. This would suggest what Siena and Jack suspected that Green the lost poet was dead and what they experienced in the tower was a ghost.

The fighting was in progress when Laura returned; the vampires seemed to be everywhere until Laura cast a spell that drew them more together like a magnet. Count Vermont was fighting Siena, they were kicking and throwing objects at each other. Jack was trying to help but knocked to the ground with the Counts mighty powerful force, he lay holding his head dazed by the blow to the head and winded by a kick to the stomach. Laura drew the other vampire's right in order to finally destroy them. Tom and Fargo were the main vampire slayers although other people joined in finding wooden stakes from broken chairs and other furniture. At last they were winning the battle as the last few vampires turned to dust and vanished. Siena was suddenly cornered by the Count he was about to kill Siena with her own stake when Tom shot an arrow into his heart, he dropped the stake and Siena picked it up. She made sure that she actually killed the Count by plunging the stake into him; she forced it deeply then watched him slowly disintegrate. The vampire leader was finally dead, at that moment the lost poet returned he noticed Lily first then the others. Fargo suddenly raced towards Siena in a rage brandishing a stake.

"There is one vampire left" Fargo shouted.

Tom reacted by shooting an arrow over Fargo's shoulder and Laura shielded Siena with her body, the arrow deflected off the wall. Laura fell to the ground as she had been stabbed in the back and was bleeding, Bramble dropped a spear and with all the confusion he had escaped and headed for the woods. Laura passed away in the arms of Siena her last words were for King Robert.

"Siena help the king restore his kingdom and forgive Fargo because he fears you" She yelled in pain "Burn my body and scatter my ashes beside a rock by the stream" with those words the witch died.

The bell tolled at the church announcing the return of the surviving villagers and the death of Count Vermont and his vampires.

Jack explained to Fargo about Siena becoming human again at that moment Faith appeared.

"God is pleased with you Siena and you can remove the bracelets and return to the church with the items that you collected for you are human again".

After fulfilling Laura's wishes and seeing the Kingdom restored Siena and Jack said their goodbyes and returned through the time portal into the art gallery, the guard was still stood confused by the painting as if they had just left. Siena and Jack acted as if nothing had happened; they were amused at the guards reaction as they appeared.

"How did you do that?" He asked transfixed on the painting.

"Oh it's a special painting isn't it Siena?"

"Very special" Siena replied

Siena and Jack arrived at the church, they put all the items in the font and watched as a glowing light appeared and all items vanished. Siena watched the sunlight shine through the windows of the church and for the first time for a long while was no longer afraid of the daylight for she was indeed human again. The bracelet fell from her wrist and she embraced jack, kissing him tenderly on the lips.

BLOOD TRAIL
PART TWO –
THE HARVEST

REVENGE OF THE VAMPIRES

It was a warm winter evening and all was calm and peaceful, Siena was preparing to go out with Jack visiting a local restaurant. She began applying the make up and suddenly saw something in the mirror, it was her reflection but as a child. She looked so sweet and innocent combing her hair and singing to herself, but then she changed into a vampire. Siena jumped and almost fell off her chair, yelling and waving her arms about. Jack was in the room and noticed her reaction, he ran towards her and hugged her.

"What is it?" Jack asked

"A vampire in the mirror" Siena said panicking.

"Siena don't be silly they don't have reflections do they?" Jack said reassuring her.

"No we don't" Siena thought for a moment "No they don't"

"You have been cured it wouldn't be you anyway" Jack said positively.

"So what was it some kind of warning? Siena asked

"We killed all the vampires remember including Count Vermont" Jack explained "Everyone died all but that weasel Bramble who fled to the woods"

"Yes your right they did" Siena said calming down "And I am no longer a vampire".

"No so why don't you carry on getting ready, we are supposed to be celebrating the day we met two years ago today" Jack said kissing her on the lips.

Once they were ready they walked out of the door, Siena did her usual thing of looking up and down the street before leaving the building. Then looked up at the sky where she noticed a full moon shining brightly above, she clung hold of Jacks hand and then grabbed his arm.

"Siena your very nervous tonight" Jack said feeling her pinching his arm

"It's a full moon" Siena said still looking up.

"You are not a vampire" Jack insisted "You're just like me, or maybe not just like me"

"I can't help feeling something is going to happen" Siena said looking at Jack.

They continued walking down the street towards the restaurant unaware that a figure was behind them, it was the shape of a man who was keeping a safe distance away.

Siena and Jack entered the restaurant and were taken by the waiter to a suitable table by the window.

"I really can't believe that it's been two year's since we met, I can still remember clearly you jumping out of the picture from that time portal" Jack said looking up from his menu.

But Siena was not paying attention; instead she was looking out of the window expecting something to happen.

"Siena are you listening to me?" Jack asked

"Yes of course" Siena said looking at the menu.

"I said, I can't believe that it's been twelve months since we met" Jack repeated himself.

"Oh yes the time portal thing" Siena said still not really paying attention "Fell into your arms"

"Oh good I am glad you figured that one out" Jack said sarcastically.

"Look I am sorry but something is going to happen tonight" Siena insisted.

At that moment they both heard sirens and noticed vehicles with flashing lights passing them by outside the window.

"Coincidence" Jack said dismissively.

"Really, you wouldn't believe it even if it hit you on your dumb head" Siena said getting up to leave.

"Siena, where are you going?" Jack said with surprise

"Out there Jack to see for myself" Siena said heading for the door.

"But, what about our meal?" He said

"Shove it Jack I am no longer hungry" She left the restaurant and walked toward the area where the vehicles went.

A crowd of people were circling a body in what was once considered a quiet and peaceful side of town. Siena pushed through some of the crowd and noticed a girl lying on the ground, her body was pale and lifeless as if she was drained of blood.

Jack noticed Siena and stood next to her; he looked at body in front of him and then glanced at Siena.

"Now will you believe me?" Siena said angrily.

"A traffic accident, why would you think that was about you?" Jack asked

"Oh Jack you idiot look at her neck, look at the puncture marks" Siena pointed.

"She has been attacked by a vampire" Jack said not thinking.

Almost everybody heard what was said, people began to talk amongst each other speaking about vampires as if they didn't exists and that Jack was some sort of mad man, but people had gone missing over the last few years to their knowledge. Strange events such as people being abducted by men and women in dark armour glowing with a green light that appeared aluminous, taken in the daylight as well as night. They were abducted from trains, changing rooms in stores and even toilets; others were taken from barn's and forest's.

The crowd were gossiping about Jack as he spoke about vampires

"He said she has been bitten by a vampire what an idiot" She said

"He ought to be locked up" Said a man laughing.

Jack walked away embarrassed with what he had said, he was unable to speak due to the shame and humiliation. Siena ran after him shouting, trying to get him to stop and face her, but he kept on walking.

"Jack stop please" She shouted.

The suddenly she felt something hit her in the shoulder, she fell to the ground with the force of the impact. Jack looked back to see her fall down, he then noticed a vampire looking right at him with her fangs showing. She was about to attack him when something shot past him, it was a stake fired from a bow that hit the vampire and she disintegrated.

"Siena" Jack shouted.

He knelt down to help her, then noticed the blood seeping through her dress

"Jack" Came a voice from behind him

Jack looked round "Tom, but what are you doing here?"

"I followed these vampires coming through a time portal, I got one coming through and followed this one who was coming after you" Tom said pointing to the remains of a vampire cloak.

Jack looked back at Siena "She has been wounded"

"She needs help" Jack shouted "Somebody, help us"

Tom placed his hand on Jack in order to reassure him, while Jack put pressure on Siena's wounds. The police and ambulance arrived at the same time, the ambulance crew began helping Siena while the police questioned Jack and Tom.

"So what happened to this woman?" The officer asked

"She was attacked by another woman" Jack replied

"Where is she now" The officer continued

"She vanished" Jack said not knowing what to say

But Jack was more concerned with Siena's condition and was eager to get to the ambulance; the ambulance crew were busy stabilising her condition and wanted to know how she had sustained her injuries. She had an abdominal wound that needed attention; it was caused by a sharp instrument like a knife.

Siena was also reluctant to answer questions she just explained it as an angry woman running through a crowd, who attacked a woman and killed her, she tried to help the woman and also got attacked.

Jack went back to the apartment with Tom, he packed a few items for Siena and they went by car to the hospital, Jack felt guilty for not believing Siena when she explained about feeling vulnerable and feeling that something was going to happen to her. But Jack considered after the death of the evil Count Vermont that it would be an end to the vampires and that they could live their life peacefully without the threat of death looming over their heads. Neither of them felt that they needed to watch one another's back for the rest of their life, hiding in shadows on the streets at night.

FAITH RETURNS

Siena was in a single room away from other patients, staff seemed to be in and out of the room regularly checking that Siena was safe. A policeman sat outside the room and watched the corridor for any suspicious characters, Jack and Tom had not arrived and Siena was concerned for their safety. Siena was tired but as she was drifting off to sleep a bright light appeared in the middle of the room, as the light became dimmer an angel appeared dressed in white with blonde hair and carrying a large key around a rope round her waist. She was accompanied by another angel with darker caramel coloured type of skin and a matching dress.

"Faith" Siena said in a weak voice

"Siena I am sorry to see you like this, may I introduce Harmony the angel who once visited Jack" She turned to face Harmony and smiled and then looked back at Siena "I am sorry to saywhen you killed Vermont, you left a few vampires alive and they are trying to avenge their master" Faith explained

"But we thought that we destroyed all of them" Siena replied

"Some escaped in a time portal into the future, they are stronger and have protective suits and helmets like dragons or demons" Faith tried to describe them emphasising their armour all dressed in black.

"So what must I do?" Siena asked

"Don't be afraid you will be helped in the future by another angel called Serenity" Harmony said.

"Go into a time portal into the future find their weakness and destroy them, if you don't the human race will continue to be threatened by the evil of vampire" Faith could see the look of fear in Siena's eyes.

"Siena you will not be alone, watch for a blue angel known as Serenity she will guide you" Faith spoke these words and vanished

At that moment a nurse entered the room walking right up to the bed on her right hand side.

"Who were you talking to?" She asked

"No one I must have been talking in my sleep" Siena said hoping the nurse would believe her.

"Well you must have had quite a conversation" she continued "Oh yes, you have visitors Jack and Tom"

Jack entered the room full of apologies making so much fuss of Siena as he hugged and kissed her.

"So sorry my love, please forgive me" He pleaded.

"It's okay Jack there is more to tell" Siena said explain about Faith

DARIUS LARICK

It was in the year 2190 in a castle much like Count Vermont's overlooking a mountainous region, within the castle walls lived an army of vampires led by Darius Larick, Darius and his brother's Radius and Matthias swore to avenge their ancestor and former Master Vermont by killing Siena and all those who helped her. Vermont had discovered time portals in various locations of the castle and moved through time, in the future he found Darius castle and discovered far more time portals using pictures to cover them up around rooms. It also made it easier to locate them. The main hall was the main area where the vampires travelled back into the past and harvested humans from various times and used their blood to survive.

Darius paced up and down the hall with a menacing look on his pale face, he was displeased and made all his followers know it.

"How many times have I asked you to get Siena and her friends and you just make excuses" He ranted

"But master we have tried" one of the women replied

"Natasha, I want no excuses, get me that woman now!" Darius insisted

"Jessica go with her and don't forget to wear your protective suits" He advised them.

"Matthias go with them and make sure she is returned here unharmed" Darius instructed "I want to kill her myself".

"Yes Darius" Matthias said leading Natasha and Jessica into the time portal

"Radius, continue the harvest, we need more humans" Darius ordered.

"But we have just returned with many humans" Radius replied

"Silence we need more, send our armies to every location, the toilet cubicles, changing rooms in stores, barns woods and graveyards. Find me humans everywhere harvest the twenty first century and bring them back here now" Darius became very angry pointing to the many paintings in the hallway.

The vampire army prepared for their journey through time wearing their protective suits so that they could venture out in the daylight, without being destroyed by the sunlight the helmets allowed them to see out but protected them from harm. The helmets appeared to resemble demons to frighten their enemies and the body armour also served useful to prevent them being attacked by weapons. The vampires of the future had proven to be more dangerous than their ancestors and they were determined to be the master race, rulers of their age.

The vampires proved successful as they entered woods capturing humans in daylight, entering graveyards both day and night. But more astonishing was their bold attempts to apprehend people from toilet cubicles and changing rooms at busy times in shopping centres. The time portals were everywhere, vampires abducted people by coming through a time portal in a changing room and pulling or dragging them straight back through time.

A barn became a brilliant place to transfer humans from the twenty first century as was a cave in Derbyshire's peak district. People were going missing all over England no one was safe, the vampires took advantage of their ability to cross over through time ever increasing their harvest.

Meanwhile Siena was relaxing trying to get some rest in hospital, Jack and Tom returned to the apartment. All was quiet and Siena began to think about what Faith had said about the future, helping mankind as if she were a vampire slayer and for that matter where were the time portals. She spoke of them appearing in odd places such as toilet cubicles and changing rooms, how strange is that and perhaps beyond belief.

At that moment the door opened and two women entered the room wearing protective black suits, they both wore helmets but by the shape of their bodies in these suits they were definitely female.

"Jessica grab her" Natasha instructed

"She's a fighter" Jessica said trying to stop Siena struggling.

"We need to put her out" Natasha said taking an instrument from her bag

"Hold her while I use this" Natasha continued "Matthias we need your help" she shouted.

Eventually Siena passed out and Matthias carried her into the female toilets, Natasha and Jessica followed behind him. They entered the second cubicle and vanished behind the cistern into the time portal and returning to Darius.

Jack and Tom returned to the hospital amongst the chaos police, nurses and other people running about. Jack entered Siena's room and noticed her missing the bedclothes were on the floor and all the equipment that she was attached to was dismantled. Then he noticed a blood trail leading to the door and followed it out of the room, he caught Tom's arm and shouted.

"Follow me Tom!" Jack led Tom into the female toilet

Tom had noticed the blood trail and assumed it belonged to Siena, they tried the first cubical but more blood led to the second cubical.

"Jack in here" Tom shouted

A woman entered the toilet "Excuse me this is the ladies toilet" she said entering the second cubicle and finding it empty "I must stop eating cheese, its causing hallucination's"

Jack and Tom went through the time portal and arrived in a strange room full of dolls, each doll looked realistic some resembled famous singers of the twenty first century others were just like Barbie dolls dressed in various outfits. One doll looked gothic with jet black hair and black lip stick, wearing dark clothes mainly dresses. Tom picked one of them up but dropped it when it spoke moving away from it walking backwards.

"It won't harm you, it's not real" Jack said reassuringly

"It's evil magic or witchcraft" Tom replied

"It's a toy doll" Jack said laughing "We have many kinds in our century, they could have got them from the twenty first century".

"Whatever you say" Tom replied

"Let's go and find Siena" Jack said heading towards a door

They walked down a corridor with stone walls either side, the corridor seemed to go on forever, and finally they reached the end noticing a large hallway in front of them, people were talking and others were appearing out of paintings. Vampires were bringing humans back from the past each of them were bound with leather ropes, every one of them looked frightened, but there was no sign of Siena. Jack and Tom remained hidden until everyone had left the hall, they moved cautiously into the hallway and then down another corridor. Jack noticed another blood trail and thought it might be Siena's blood, it led into a room Jack went in but Tom hesitated.

"It might be a trap Jack" Tom said concerned

"Nonsense it's fine I think it's another time portal" Jack replied

At that moment Tom was pushed into the room and a door slammed shut behind him.

"One day Jack you may listen to others" Tom said disappointedly

A face appeared at the door, the man seemed pleased with himself

"Now I have Jack and Siena, I will be able to avenge my master" Darius said laughing

"How do you know me?" Jack asked

"A little man called Bramble told me of you, he is right here do you wish to see him?" Darius asked pushing Brambles face up to a key hole in the door.

"Bramble you sly worm always willing to betray others" Tom shouted

"Yes Bramble you're a murderer killing Laura" Jack shouted

"Get your stinking body away from here" Tom shouted

"Well Bramble you're not very well liked" Darius said "Perhaps Siena will greet you more favourably"

"Keep away from Siena!" Jack shouted "I am warning you"

"Such empty threats Jack, you have no weapons you are defenceless and you threaten us" Darius said goading him "You will die soon enough I will feed you to my children"

Siena had been taken to another part of the castle far away from Jack and Tom, she was alone, but in a nicely decorated room with a four poster bed and red curtains all around it. She wore a fine dress and her hair was platted neatly, she was able to see Darius on a monitor on the wall.

"Do you propose to kill me" Siena asked

"Call me Darius" He relied "Frankly I admire your courage"

"Darius Larick" She said calmly "I have heard of you, leader of the vampires"

Darius had dark thick hair which he swept back and revealed scars on his cheeks and chin, his eyes were menacing and his complexion was pale almost white.

"Count Vermont needs to be avenged and some of my flock are from his castle, they want you to die, but you should die the death of a vampire, driven into the light to disintegrate. Your death will be slow and painful as the vampires wish it, but we need to change you back into a vampire first and then execute you". Darius explained.

"A vampire once more?" Siena asked "I am to be bitten again"

"Yes and starve for a while then your boyfriend Jack can join you and be the first to be drained of blood by you" Darius smiled "You will destroy him and then we will destroy you"

Siena walked around the room thinking, her thoughts returned to the days her mother used to read stories to her, while her father was out hunting vampires. She and her sister woke up many nights hearing wolves crying out with owl and other wild creatures making noises. Sometimes storms kept them awake the sound of wind blowing through trees or thunder banging in the skies, and heavy rain thrashing again the windows. But then Siena missed the walks through the meadows and stepping through streams with her naked feet, the sun beating down upon her as she rode her horse into the village. All these memories and no one to share them with she was alone, sad and feeling helpless, then she remember Faith and all she said to her.

"God I need you now help me fight this wickedness" she prayed

Suddenly the room was filled with a blue light and an angel appeared she was dressed in blue, a long dress even her hair was pale blue. She looked amazing, her face expressed a calmness never seen before and instantly she made Siena feel good.

"I am called Serenity I am an angel sent to help you" She said

"Faith spoke of you in the future" Siena said

"Time has no relevance to us, we are timeless" Serenity replied

"I wish I could say the same" She said looking into her blue eyes

"You seem different to Faith" Siena observed

"We appear differently to all mankind, they see what they want to see or understand, we can be white, black, brown look like any nationality, race or creed" Serenity demonstrated by changing her appearance.

"That's amazing" Siena said surprised

"Even animals if it is necessary" Serenity explained with another demonstration as a white cat followed by a dog.

"Now I am really freaked out" She said shaking her head

"But you want to know how to defeat the vampires" she said bringing Siena back to reality "Firstly you need to escape from here"

"That's impossible" Siena said negatively

"Have Faith Siena and believe in miracles for one is about to occur" She said making the door open with the wave of her hand.

"I will be stopped by vampires" Siena said looking towards the door

"You will be invisible to them, just follow my blue light which will lead you out of the castle and to Carina the vampire slayer". She said reassuringly.

"Follow the blue light and that's it?" Siena said apprehensively.

"Trust in god and follow the light, don't take your eyes off it for one minute or you will be seen" Serenity advised.

With those words Serenity disappeared followed by a blue ball of light resembling an orb, it began moving forward towards the door. Siena followed it as instructed and it continued down the corridor past the main hall and towards the main door, the door opened and she was free. Although she had escaped the castle, she was still not safe and so she continued to follow the blue light into the woods, even now she was transfixed on the light which travelled through the trees and suddenly disappeared.

"Great the lights gone out, did the battery go or something?" Siena said baffled.

"Siena" came a female voice

Siena turned around slowly and came face to face with a woman wearing dark armour and long dark hair, she was attractive with dark complexion and hazel eyes.

"I saw the guiding light and was instructed by an angel to look out for you" She said extending her arm forward with her hand open "I am Carina"

Siena shook her by the hand "I am obviously Siena"

"You are either brave or stupid coming here to fight with us against the wicked vampire leader Darius Larick" Carina said smiling.

"I would probably choose stupid as I am no warrior" she replied

"I would say brave, we can teach you to fight, besides your name is legend in history" she said hoping to instil confidence in her.

"I sincerely hope your right Carina" Siena said smiling back at her

"Let us go and meet the rest of my soldiers" She said leading the way

As they walked along they were joined by other soldiers both male and female each carrying weapons.

"The vampires don't tend to challenge us too much as we have weapons that they know are harmful to them, they generally keep their distance. Carina explained and then paused for a moment "However now you are with us they may try to attack us in order to get you back"

At that moment the sound of branches breaking broke the silence and vampires were instantly upon them, encircling them some flying like bats.

"Stand your ground men" Carina instructed

The vampires attacked using swords and other bladed instruments, swinging them and hitting their enemy. Blood spurted in the air and the sound of clashing steal drowned out the cries of wounded soldiers from the opposing armies. It was a battle to the death and no one at this stage was winning, not until Carina took out her weapon and shot one of the vampires blasting away the armour from his chest and exposing his body to daylight. He immediately disintegrated and Carina used the same weapon on another vampire, and then continued to use it until the vampire realised they would be defeated and fled.

"That will teach those evil bastards" Carina said confidently

"You really showed them Carina" a male soldier said

"Yes another victory to us I think" Carina boasted

They travelled further through streams and a forest until they reached a modern building, Carina placed her right hand on a panel and a light shone into her right eye. The door opened sliding to the left and allowed everyone in, the section that they were in was a main control area with a series of machinery including computers and armoury.

People were walking about everywhere some in white boiler suits each seemed to have a purpose or job to do, it was more high tech than Siena expected but then she did originate from the Seventh century.

Carina led Siena into a large conference room where she debriefed her army, making sure that Siena was included in the meeting.

"For those who do not know, this is Siena" she put her arm around Siena

"She is a legend from the seventh century who destroyed Count Vermont and made her name in history as a vampire slayer" Carina continued "We have the honour of being in her presence at a crucial time in our champagne to rid the world of these evil vampires"

"What makes you think we can trust her, after all she has been with these vampires" one man protested

"Gareth, how dare you question my judgement, have I not always led you all well, protected you and defended all of you no matter what you have done"

"Yes madam of course, but she has been with Darius Larick himself" He continued

"Look!" Carina shouted exposing both sides of her neck "Do you see any puncture wounds, scars or indications that he has turned her into a vampire, I have on good authority that she is one of us".

"A blue angel wasn't it" He mocked "She was once a vampire who was turned into a human"

"Step forward Gareth!" Carina commanded

Gareth was a large man with reseeding black hair and a face full of scars, he was a muscular man with skin like leather.

"Touch Siena, feel her neck, check her teeth and please expose her to light, you can even get a mirror and see if you can see her refection". Carina encouraged him to test her knowing that she was not a vampire.

Gareth examined her neck as instructed and then proceeded to open her mouth

"Are you satisfied" Carina asked him

"Yes okay I was wrong about her, but I am only saying what the rest are thinking" Gareth admitted

Carina became enraged at his remark and struck him in the face with her studded gloved fist, this was followed by a kick to the throat.

"How, dare you challenge me like this, do you all think of me this way, I have offered you a solution to the evil of the vampires" She watched Gareth wiping the blood from his face and struggling to talk "Let that be a lesson to all of you not to undermine my authority or question my judgment"

"So what now Carina" one of the female soldiers said reluctantly for fear of being attacked

"Now" Carina hesitated feeling that she had actually gone too far "Now we rest and consider our next move".

NATASHA

It seemed like an eternity that Jack and Tom had been imprisoned, they had had many conversations but had exhausted every subject and became silent. Darius had listened in and was disappointed because none of the subjects were relevant to him and his cause.

"Natasha my dear, you must convince Jack that Siena has died and console him, make him trust you and he could provide you with valuable information" Darius explained

"Yes of course master" Natasha said in a humble manner

"Damn, what was that blue light that led Siena out of here, how the hell did she escape my clutches" Darius lifted his head and spread out his arms "Let the greatness of our kind defeat the human race, let us harvest more souls and drink the blood of our victims".

The main hall filled with human bodies "Feast to our future take the blood from these people". Darius commanded watching the vampires swoop down upon a crowd of screaming humans.

The vampires pinned their victims down and pierced their necks with their sharp fangs sucking their blood and draining them of life. The vampires would not rest until they had feasted enough to satisfy their needs, all that was left was limp carcasses sprawled all across the hall.

Both Jack and Tom heard the cries and could see on the monitor what had occurred, so many deaths all for the sake of blood, these people had come from the twenty first century, abducted and brought through the time portals. They knew that in time it would be them who would be victims and they had no way of fighting them unarmed. Their fate rested in the arms of the vampires who had no love for humans, their only desire was to feast off humans and drain them of their blood. Suddenly they were both disturbed by the opening of the cell, a number of vampires wearing armour entered the room, Tom rushed forward to fight them off but they were too strong and pushed Tom over. They wanted Jack so left Tom on the floor and dragged Jack out of the room, Jack was too weak to fight them off and went along with them quietly. He was taken to the same room that Siena once stayed, the vampires dropped him on the bed like a sack of potatoes, and he was curled up in a foetal position all alone and vulnerable.

After a while the door opened and a woman walked in dressed in a long flowing silk dress, she walked up to the edge of the bed and watched him for a while. Then she walked closer to him and touched his head with her hand, stroking his forehead and whispering down his ear.

"Jack are you awake" She asked

Jack opened his eyes to the most beautiful woman that he had ever seen, her eyes were hypnotic just like Siena's used to be when she was a vampire, she was slim with a flawless complexion and flowing blonde hair. She was like an angel and yet could have been the devil in disguise, charming and seductive, with a type of cunning grin that told Jack to be cautious.

"Who are you?" He finally muttered

"I am Natasha, I need to talk to you" She said sitting on the bed

"I am afraid that I have some bad news for you" Natasha began to look sad

"What is it?" Jack asked

"It's about Siena" She continued diverting her eyes away from him

"Siena where is she?" Jack asked concerned

"She is dead" She replied not wanting to face him

"You're lying you're a vampire, she's not dead" Jack said in disbelief.

"Why would I lie?" She said calmly

"But how did she die?" Jack tried to find reason with what she had said "Did you kill her?"

"No, died from her wounds, we tried to save her after all she was once a vampire" Natasha was trying to reason with Jack "We wanted her alive"

She looked at Jack with tears in her eyes holding him and watching him crumble in her arms, she kissed him on the right cheek and gazed into his eyes.

"Jack please be brave you must survive, I can help you, look into my eyes" she said beginning to hypnotise him. "Feel my love, my compassion tell me what you are feeling right now"

Jack began to murmur but not make any sense, he felt out of control as his body began to weaken and he fell back on the bed. Natasha watched his heart beating beneath his chest and his neck was exposed and ready for her to bite.

"Let me kiss you" She said revealing her fangs

Natasha was close to Jacks neck, she had punctured his neck when suddenly she was disturbed by another person in the room, Natasha drew away from Jack with spectacles of blood on her teeth.

"Natasha leave him for now we have other work to do" the person said

"Jessica what are you doing, Darius wants me to seduce him for information" Natasha said angrily

"But it is Darius who sent for you" Jessica replied

"Damn and I was just enjoying myself" she said cursing

The next morning Jack woke up and began to look around the room, then he touched his neck as it felt so uncomfortable. He could feel the puncture wounds made from her fangs and began to panic, he struggled to his feet and looked in the mirror only to find tiny holes with hardly any penetration. But he could still have been converted into a vampire but he was looking at his own reflection in the mirror. So no evidence of being a vampire and he didn't feel weak as if he had lost a lot of blood, maybe he had a lucky escape this time although he couldn't imagine why.

Natasha looked angrily at Darius "Why did you stop me!"

"My child I merely wanted you to seduce him not change him into a vampire" Darius said calmly

"I was getting somewhere and he would be a worthy adversary against the slayers" She replied "You don't trust me do you".

Darius became furious and struck Natasha knocking her to the floor, she began crawling away from him, wiping her mouth as she went.

"No one disobeys their master, I will not hear of it" Darius watched her leave the hall and turned his attention to Matthias.

"I am in command and will be respected" He said waiting for a reaction from Matthias.

Darius took a goblin which was filled with fresh blood and drank from it, he passed it to Matthias who too drank from it and in turn offered it to Jessica.

"We drink the blood of human's in a pact to destroy all slayers" Darius gazed around the room at his followers.

Each person nodded in turn acknowledging their agreement with their gestures, and then they all began to converse.

"Matthias you are my most loyal subject, tell me what do you think of Natasha?" Darius asked.

"She is not to be trusted"

Later that evening Natasha returned to see Jack, she appeared nervous as she stood in front of Jack, he was apprehensive after her last visit and backed away from her "I just wanted to apologise for my actions"

"But you bit me what was that all about?" He asked "I have puncture wounds on my neck, am I now a vampire or what?"

"No" she replied "I didn't even suck your blood"

"So why have you returned?" Jack asked

"Come closer I need to tell you something" she beckoned.

"So that you can do the same again or worse" he replied

"Trust me I want to help you" she said trying to get closer.

She whispered to him "Siena is alive"

"What?" Jack asked with disbelief

"Look at me please" Natasha pleaded "Siena is alive, she escaped somehow"

"I don't understand" Jack was trying to make sense of the situation

"I want to help you" Natasha repeated

"Then help me to escape" Jack still didn't trust her but he considered that he had nothing to lose.

"Okay, but tell me that we would have been good together and kiss me just once passionately" she appeared to be genuine when she made her request.

"Alright just once and that's it" Jack agreed

"Just once" she said kissing him on the lips

Natasha pulled away and moved towards the door, the monitor had been disconnected and Natasha hit the camera with a weapon that she had dropped on the floor near the door.

"Come quickly" she pleaded "We don't have much time"

Jack ran towards her and followed her into the corridor, he paused for a moment "I need to help Tom"

"There is no time, come on" she said becoming anxious

"Not without Tom" Jack insisted

"Very well" she agreed

They went to Tom's cell and freed him while the vampires were still feasting, Tom was relieved that Jack was back and hugged him.

"Thank god you're safe" he said smiling "But who is she?"

"She is our escape plan, get out of jail free" Jack said smiling back

"Come on" Natasha pleaded

They headed down the corridor and towards the door, but as they opened it, the light shone in and Natasha ran back into the corridor. Jack ran into a room and took a bed spread off the bed, then returned and covered Natasha up.

"Right, now let's go" Jack said

They raced outside and headed into the woods, they seemed to travel for hours and before long it began to get dark.

After a further two hours they reached Carina's base and confronted the slayers, Natasha expected hostility as she was the enemy and as a vampire she was a predator.

"Why is she here?" Carina asked

"Natasha helped me escape" Jack explained

"But she's a vampire" Carina said

At that point Siena came in the room and ran straight towards Jack

"Jack!" she shouted "You're alive and Tom" she noticed the puncture marks on his neck "What's this Jack, what happened?"

"It's not what you think Siena" Jack said in his defence

"It's a bite, a vampire bite" Siena said concerned

"I did it but he's okay" Natasha admitted

Siena slapped her across the face so hard that she fell backwards

"Why is she here?" Siena shouted "She is a vampire who even attacked you"

"But she helped us escape" Jack explained "Maybe she can help us"

"No way, not possible" Gareth said "I don't need a vampire helping me, it's bad enough with Siena here"

"Who is the big guy?" Jack asked "Why is he so pissed off with Siena?"

"Because I am an ex vampire" Siena said dismissing Gareth

"And who are you?" Carina asked Tom

"I am a vampire slayer from the seventh century" Tom said "I was like you Gareth, I thought Siena was an evil vampire until I saw her kill Count Vermont. Now I feel the same about Natasha, but as Jack said she helped me and she has knowledge of the vampires and the layout of the castle".

"So we can rescue the humans in the castle and destroy the vampires" Jack said

"I can destroy the time portals too" Siena said positively

"Wait a second" Carina said turning towards Siena and Jack "It's as simple as that, we have a lot of planning to do"

"While you are planning people are dying, doesn't anybody care" Siena said holding back her tears "They are murderers and harvesters of humans from the twenty first century, they drain them of blood and discard their carcases like wild animals" she said looking at Natasha.

"We can't just go in there and attack vampires" Carina replied "It would be suicide and as for rescuing humans that too requires planning".

"Each day we waste another life is lost, they drain the blood from humans and destroy lives" Siena said disturbed.

"Oh, so you never did this Siena" Gareth shouted "You never sucked the blood out of a human as a vampire"

"Yes, but I was confused and deeply regret what I did" Siena said defending herself.

"You still did it" Gareth went on "Lives were lost so that you could live"

"That's enough Gareth this is getting us nowhere" Carina butted in "Natasha knows the layout of the castle so let's start there"

"Natasha is going to help us?" Siena asked feeling uncomfortable in her presence

"Well she helped me escape" Jack said defending her

"She also bit you or have you forgotten that" Siena said pointing to his neck

"We discussed this and the circumstances which led to this" Jack said

"Oh and that makes it alright, she can just go around biting people at will, or does she fancy you" Siena turned her back on Jack and walked away.

The next few days consisted of training to fight the vampires, Siena wanted to use Natasha as a punch bag in order to practice kick boxing, but Carina kept Natasha away from her. In fact Natasha stayed with Carina in order to plan the attack on the castle and help the humans in captivity, she was conscious of Natasha's fondness towards Jack, but needed her to get them back into the castle.

Natasha caught Jack going back to his room in the evening, he looked tired and was about to rejoin Siena.

"Jack" She whispered "Please don't return to the castle it's too dangerous"

"I have to I need to help the humans" Jack replied

"But you know the danger and we could go somewhere else together" She gripped his arm "Let's forget all these people and start again"

"Natasha you know I can't do this I am with Siena" he explained

"I want to be human, seek god like Siena did" she gazed into his eyes "You told me she made a deal with god to be human"

"Siena had to do so many tasks and destroy Count Vermont" Jack said stepping away from her.

"Then I will destroy Darius" She replied anxiously "And tell you the secret of the time portals"

"Wait, you know the secret of the time portals?" Jack hesitated

"Yes it is all about a girl called Lily, she holds the secret" She said waiting for a response from Jack.

"Lily a girl with ginger hair and pointed ears about seven years old?" he asked

Natasha laughed "Sorry but you haven't quite grasped the concept of time travel, little Lily is twenty now and continues to travel through time".

"All this time, so she grew up?" Jack asked

"Naturally" Natasha replied "We don't stay children forever"

"But it seems like five minutes since we went there" Jack said astonished

"She discovered the first time portals and knows how to close them, that's how we come to travel from place to place" She explained

"But what about Lily is she now a vampire?" Jack asked concerned

"No, no one will harm her because of the time portals, if anything happened to upset her metabolism it could affect the portals and restrict vampire movement" she said "But Siena should know that being a vampire"

"Ex vampire" Jack remarked "Maybe it was not known by the seventh century vampires, she didn't appear to know about time portals when we first met and she came from one then"

"Lily likes dolls she gathers them from various locations in time and brings them back here to her dolls room, some look so real, some talk" Natasha explained "Find the dolls and Lily is close by like a dolls trail"

At that moment the door opened and Siena stood looking cross at them both, Jack picked up her signal and said goodnight to Natasha.

"So, what did she want, was it to bite your neck again?" Siena asked sarcastically

"As a matter of fact she was telling me about Lily" Jack said not wishing to say anything about Natasha's desire to run away with him.

"Lily?" Siena asked "How does she know Lily?"

Jack explained to her about the time portals and the dolls, she appeared to be listening and absorbing the information until he mentioned her age.

"Twenty that's impossible we left her a few years ago" she said in disbelief

"It is something about time travel and portals" Jack tried to explain

"Nonsense she is trying to trick you and I wouldn't be surprised if she doesn't try to seduce you again or try to carry you off somewhere" Siena said as if she had heard their conversation.

"Well she is trying to help us enter the castle and rescue the human prisoners" Jack said in her defence.

"I don't trust her, she is out for her own desires" Siena said "But you take it all in like a sponge, both you and Carina"

The next night the slayers were ready to go to the castle, Jack had related to Tom about Lily and the time portals. Tom reminded Jack about the dolls room and how the dolls looked, Jack was so anxious about Siena he had not noticed the dolls expressions or voices. I was almost as if the room was alive, and all due to Lily who had collected and dressed them so elegantly. Siena remained quiet watching Natasha's every move in case she betrayed them, although she trusted Jack with her life she considered him a little gullible at times. She cast her mind back on the time when she wanted to turn him into a vampire and attempted to bite him, he was shocked at the time and he felt uneasy in her company for a time. Woman are a complex sex most of the time but enhanced when they are also vampires with a motive in mind, Siena could see this and was acting upon her instincts being cautious of Natasha.

They arrived at the castle, Natasha managed to get inside and let the slayers in, and they crept down a dark corridor towards the dungeons. Natasha led them down some stone steps spiralling around a wall, everyone seemed uneasy until they reached the bottom, suddenly there was shouting coming from the dark.

"Attack them!" the voice shouted

Vampires seemed to appear everywhere attacking the slayers, Natasha turned on Siena knocking her to the ground and hissing at her showing her vampire fanged teeth and clawing at her with her sharp nails. Matthias stood watching his vampires as they slaughtered many of the slayers, they had all been ambushed and betrayed by Natasha who managed to arrange the trap for them. Siena was injured but determined to fight back with all she had, with blood on her clothes and blood dripping from fresh wounds, kicking Natasha and causing her to stumble, Carina lurched forward and administered the final fatal blow piercing her chest with a stake and watching as she disintegrated. She turned to Gareth and ordered the slayers to retreat, not many survived on this occasion as they ran into the forest.

"Damn!" Gareth shouted "I told you she would betray us"

But no one even replied to him just let him rant on to himself and calm down as he travelled home licking his wounds like lion after a feast. When they arrived home the other slayers help them bath their cuts and encouraged them to rest. Some of them mourned their friends and relatives who died so gallantly in the castle, while the vampires feasted on the humans blood and celebrated their victory.

It was weeks before Carina planned another rescue mission into the castle, in fact the vampires thought that the slayers had left the area. They sent vampires out to investigate but they were cautious due to the weapons that the slayers possessed. They were far superior to their own and unbeknown to the slayers could wipe out the vampires with one swift attack, so the vampires concentrated on their harvest and continued to abduct humans from the twenty first century. They at least knew how vulnerable they were and how easy they could snatch them and return them to the castle via the time portals. Meanwhile Carina set up a training program for her remaining slayers teaching them how to defend themselves including Siena and Jack. She also educated them in the new weaponry using swords, guns containing special chemicals in the bullets and a type of hand grenade that would blast away their armour. A month passed Siena was becoming quite a warrior virtually matching the skills of Carina who was a modern Boudica or Joan of Arc, they also became close friends which didn't please Gareth as he was still apposed to Siena and failed to trust her even though she fought so gallantly in the last battle. Siena and Carina practiced fighting together and often shared a meal even Jack felt left out and spent his time with Tom discussing combat strategies. But Siena's real challenge was against Gareth as they fought in a ring using weapons and hand to hand combat. Gareth nearly killed Siena striking out with a sword, Tom stopped him and Siena actually caught his arm and held a sword to his throat.

"If I wanted to kill you I would have done before now" She had broken the skin on his neck "But I think you're a great warrior and under that rock of muscles a nice man"

Gareth bowed his head and actually smiled and then looked at Carina "Maybe I was wrong about her"

Carina smiled back "You big soft Gorilla" she said winking at Siena

Later everyone assembled in the main area and Carina addressed the audience

"My fellow slayers we have been through much together, we have battled with the evil vampires and been betrayed by Natasha, this time we will be ready to defeat the them and free the humans that are captured. There harvest will be over and the time portals will be sealed preventing any of them to ever harvest again, this will end the evil that they have bestowed upon us and we shall be free once more".

"Let us do battle and then celebrate our victory together" Gareth said proudly.

THE FINAL BATTLE

It was a dark and dismal night, the moon was full and an army of slayers had said their fair wells to friends and relatives as they made their way to the castle for the final battle, hopefully to end the evil that has fallen on the human race. But the slayers are equipped with new weaponry and have been training for this final conquest against the vampires even though the vampires have black protective armour that gives off a glowing green light like emeralds. They also use electrical charges like taser guns powerful enough to stun people, they used these to capture humans in the twenty first century. But will these match the mighty weapons that the slayer had, it was highly doubtful as they possessed weapons that could blast away their armour and destroy the vampires in one single shot. One of the slayers went out one evening and hunted down vampires using such weapons and destroyed them this is what the vampires feared but never anticipated a full assault on the castle.

The slayers entered the castle using the north and south walls, Siena and Jack went with Carina while Tom went to the south wall with Gareth. The plan was to infiltrate the castle from both ends and meet in the great hall, and then when the vampires were defeated they would release the prisoners and return them to their own time. The plan was going well Gareth and Tom had destroyed the vampires from the south section and was heading towards the great hall. Some of the vampires led by Radius and Jessica fled through one of the time portals, hoping to escape their ultimate fate. Darius was busy fighting Gareth, while Matthias was battling with Carina, Siena was fighting off some of the female vampires close by. Few vampires were left but one managed to fatally wound Tom penetrating his back with a sword, he dropped to the ground and Siena ran to his rescue, but he was too late Tom was already dying. Jack saw what had happened and also ran to his aid, Jack held his head from the back of the neck.

"Have we beaten them?" He asked

"Yes, we are the victors" Jack replied

"Please say hello to Lily for me" Tom said

"Come on Tom, you can say it yourself" Jack replied

Darius flew towards Jack after he had wounded Gareth, Siena aimed her gun at Darius and blasted a hole through his armour and he disintegrated. Carina continued to fight Matthias and finally defeated him with a few shots using her special bullets, he too disintegrated into dust.

The slayers had finally defeated all the vampires in the castle and the humans were freed and sent home via the time portals. Siena and Jack knew their next journey was through the time portal in search of Lily and hopefully close the time portals for good.

IN SEARCH OF LILY

Siena stood beside Carina both tired from the battle and both looking around

"I never thought I would see this, standing here surrounded by the armour of dead vampires" Carina said

"I was beginning to think we would die" Siena admitted

"Some vampires escaped" Carina seemed concerned

"Don't worry Carina we will find them" Siena said confidently

"I will have this area guarded twenty four hours, no one will return here" Carina said determined to stop the vampires returning via the time portals.

"I am sure they won't come back" Siena said looking at the paintings

"So what will you do now?" Carina asked her

"Find Lily and secret to the time portals" Siena replied "Then seek the vampires that escaped"

"Well, I wish you luck Siena" Carina said embracing her "Thank you" she said kissing her on the cheek.

Siena and Jack slept at the castle that night in order to rest before finding Lily, Jack was very restless in bed while Siena despite being tired found it hard to sleep. Her mind was active and drifting back to her experiences in the seventeenth century, surviving in Vermont's castle as a vampire and running around with her sister Emma as children. During the time she was reflecting on her past a bright blue light glowed in the room and Serenity the blue angel appeared so stunningly beautiful dressed in a long blue dress.

"Siena you have done well to defeat the evil reign of the vampires" she said

"But I was helped and some still live" Siena said humbly

"You will find them; they went into a time portal some to the seventeenth century and others to the twenty first century" she replied

"I will search for them and destroy the rest of the evil" Siena said

With that Serenity vanished and left Siena feeling brighter and able to sleep, despite Jack thrashing around and mumbling in his sleep. Clearly he was still fighting vampires as he occasionally yelled out punching the pillow with his fists.

The next morning Siena and Jack said their farewells and headed for the doll's room in order to find the time portal and seek Lily. On entering the room they noticed the doll's, Jack was more attentive and remembered that Tom considered them evil because they moved and spoke. This time one of the dolls moved and spoke strangely to them as if it knew them and wanted to give them a message.

"Like a person within a person, fictitious people within a dream" she said

"And nightmares keep you awake, and no one will hear you scream" said another.

"Hidden away in a fortress tower so high upon a hill" Siena said

"The lost poet" Jack said realising it was a quote from the lost poet.

"Lily read that poem" Siena said remembering her sitting at the camp fire.

"She is in the tower" Jack said realising what the doll's meant.

"A trapped talent within a cell" Siena quoted "You're right but which portal is it?"

"The picture over there of the tower, that's it let's go" Jack said excitedly.

They entered the time portal and found themselves landing on the hard stone floor of a room that was dark and mysterious.

"This floor is filthy I feel so dirty" Siena said complaining

"Clearly someone hasn't mopped or dusted recently" Jack agreed.

"So where are we?" Siena asked

"I don't know but it's creepy" Jack said deep voice

"Jack that isn't funny" Siena replied nervously

"It could be the tower where the lost poet used to write" Jack said pondering

"Oh how horrid!" Siena shrieked

"What?" Jack replied

"I can feel something over my face like a cob web or something" She spitted something out of her mouth "I can taste it"

"How horrid" Jack said teasing her

"Jack stop it and look for a door" Siena insisted

"Found it" Jack said happily

"What was that bang?" Siena asked

"My bloody head, I hit it on the door frame" Jack said rubbing his forehead

They entered a dark corridor Siena held Jacks hand and they proceeded to walk down slowly, watching out for obstacles in their pathway.

"I hate this Jack" Siena said her hands were sweating and she was quivering.

"So do I" Jack admitted

They walked further and suddenly Siena let out a scream as something dropped on her head, she was becoming hysterical, it was wet and slimy and seemed to drop from the ceiling. Jack tried to identify it but it was too dark to see it clearly but it was motionless, if it had been living it was dead now.

"What the hell was that?" Siena asked Jack

"I don't know but it isn't living" Jack replied kicking it "Lets move on"

As they journeyed on they saw a light ahead of them, Jack began to wonder whether or not he had been dreaming this experience, he had questioned whether the time travel had affected his mind and distorted every thought he had, he was unable to differentiate fact from fiction. Reality from dreams which made him think even the vampires were unreal, perhaps the whole experience with meeting Siena in the art gallery was a dream. But this would mean Siena didn't exist and the here and now was a dream or nightmare. As they entered the lighted area Jack noticed paintings on the wall and realised they had arrived in Vermont's castle but it appeared deserted, Siena gazed around and Jack began staring at her trying to decide whether or not she was real.

"Jack what's wrong?" Siena asked

"Are you real?" Jack asked

"What?" Siena asked confused

"Are you really here or are you a figment of my imagination?" Jack asked

"Imagine this" Siena slapped him so hard he stumbled over

"What was that for?" Jack asked shocked

"Of all the cheek" Siena said angrily "How dare you treat me like this"

"Like what?" Jack asked innocently

"After all we have been through you ask me if I am real" Siena began pacing

"Oh stop, when you pace you're angry and that's bad for me" Jack said worried

"Piss off Jack you moron!" Siena shouted "Go on piss off"

"But I don't know what is real anymore" Jack said defending himself

Siena kicked him in the leg "That's bloody real"

"Ouch!" Jack cried holding his leg "What was that for?"

"A reality check, there you are alive" Siena was about to say more when she was interrupted by a door banging and someone rushing down a flight of stairs. It was the hunched figure of the goblin called Bramble, he was rushing out of the castle like his trousers were on fire.

"Bramble" Jack whispered

"Is he real?" Siena asked sarcastically

"Too right he is and travelled through a time portal to here" Jack replied

"So some of the vampires must have followed" Siena said noticing Jack still rubbing his knee.

"I am sorry Jack, but you annoyed me" Siena made an effort to apologise "And I have been traumatised by that thing that dropped on my head"

"Let's forget it and find out where Bramble is going" Jack said in a forgiving manner.

They followed Bramble into the woods and soon lost him, it was as if he knew they were following him and he found a hole to hide in. Siena and Jack decided to continue down the meadow to find Fargo, they had a feeling he would be in exactly the same spot that they originally found him in by stream sitting on a rock. Sure enough the giant was there and greeted them like old friends.

"My friends welcome back" he said smiling

"My dear Fargo how are you?" Siena asked

"I am well" he looked them both up and down "You both look well, but you have never grown"

"We need to know your secret Fargo, so that we can grow like you" Jack said looking up to him

"So what brings you back here, surely not me?"

"Much as we love you Fargo, we are looking for Lily" Siena said seriously

"Ah little Lily of course" He thought

"No big Lily she is twenty now" Jack said demonstrating her height with his hand in the air.

"Lily was small when we were here seeking the vampires" Siena said

"Think we need to find the tower of the lost poet, she was fascinated by his writing, I will travel with you" Fargo offered

"Have you heard anything about the vampires?" Jack asked

"Yes, people say they have been here at night and took people away" Fargo explained.

"So they are here" Siena said "We must stop them from leaving here"

"So that's what Bramble was up to, he was doing their work for them, searching for victims and leading the vampires to them".

"You must shelter here tonight and we can go to the poet's tower tomorrow" Fargo explained directing them to his cave which was surrounded by fresh garlic.

Fargo offered them supper and a comfortable place to sleep, it was so warm and cosy unlike the vampire castle that they had left behind in the future. But although they were so comfortable in bed together, Jack continued to thrash around in the night. Jack was dreaming about Natasha trying to seduce him, she was naked and teasing him by licking his ears and telling him that she loved him. Jack tried to control his desires and begged her to leave him alone, it was then that she exposed her fangs and plunged them into his neck sucking his blood. Jack tried to fight her and she changed into Siena, he pushed her away thrashing his arms in the air and waking up yelling "No!"

When he awoke Siena was on the floor holding her face and clearly in pain, he had hit her in the face during his struggle, Siena had tried to wake him in order to stop him from dreaming and was struck by him.

"Jack you idiot" Siena shouted

"Sorry did I hit you?" he said shocked

"Too right you did with your mad dreams of vampires" she replied

"How did you know that?" Jack asked her.

"You were shouting Natasha" she replied in disgust"

"Oh" Jack replied "Sorry"

"So what was this with Natasha, did you love her?" Siena asked jealously

"No, she kept trying to seduce me and bite me, she wanted us to be together" Jack admitted

"Why didn't you tell me?" Siena asked

"I did try to when we were going back to the castle with her" Jack said hoping his excuse would be enough to silence her.

"Well you didn't tell me which makes me think you don't care about me and would have gone with her" Siena said trying to mentally beat a confession out of him.

"No never, Siena I love you and I would never have ran away with her" Jack considered himself out of trouble but Siena was not going to let him off so easily, she was an ex vampire who never allowed her prey to get away.

"So, she wanted you to run away with her, the slag" Siena was fuming she got up from the floor and started pacing like a caged animal

"I would never have done that Siena" Jack said "Please come back to bed"

"I never trusted her, she was deviant and cunning, I true vampire" Siena said turning to face him "But you trusted her"

"She had a plan of the castle, she knew the layout of the castle" He looked into her eyes "You were a vampire"

"That's different I wanted to be human" Siena began to cry in frustration

"She told me that she wanted to be human, I would have asked for your help to make it so" Jack said

"She was using you to get to me and wanted to defeat the slayers" Siena said "She wanted to please Darius to kill him and take control of the vampires as leader, that was her plan" Siena had figured it out "She used everyone including you"

Jack sat speechless just staring into space, he knew that Siena was right but couldn't help feeling that Natasha was really fond of him. Siena lay beside him and they embraced, Jack felt her warm flesh touching his and they began to make love. The night seemed to pass quickly and before long Fargo had entered the area and nudging them to wake up; They got dressed and then joined him, he had prepared breakfast on a large table.

"Please eat" He said as they both sat near him

"Thank you" They both said

"I heard arguing last night" Fargo said

"Just a disagreement" Siena replied "Nothing important really"

"We are fine" Jack agreed

It was soon time to depart Siena and Jack collected all their weapons for the trip and headed through the meadow and into the mountains where the tower stood. There it stood in front of them high upon a hill the tower that they once visited with their friends a few years ago. John Gilbert Green the lost poet disappeared and was thought to be a ghost within the tower, writing unfinished compositions, a lonely man with little known about him but his fear of ghouls and monsters caused him to hide away in the tower. He was tormented by his nightmares he could never escape from them. The poet described himself as an image with a captured soul, he had died in the tower but his soul was with the vampires only free when they had been destroyed. They entered the tower and began the long walk up the spiral stairs to the top, not knowing what to expect when they reached the top. As they entered the room nothing had changed the table stood with the parchment a jar of ink and a quill, the curtain were the same and the image of the lost poet sat near the table. Suddenly there was a crashing sound as books fell to the ground and a figure ran towards a picture, she was slim with ginger hair and pointed eyes, wearing periodic a costume of the age. She had green trousers and a white blouse with a colourful pattern, her hair was platted falling down her back. Siena shouted to her in order to stop her from entering the time portal, she paused but failed to turn around, just maintained her pose.

"Lily" Siena repeated "It's me Siena, I need your help"

Lily remained motionless listening to what was being said to her, Siena moved forward as she continued to speak to her in an attempt to hold her back from the portal.

"Listen Lily the vampires are using the time portals to transport humans into the future for harvesting, they want blood to feast on human blood like yours" Siena felt as if she was failing to get through to her, at that moment Green the lost poet ghost appeared and he began to speak.

"Listen to Siena, Lily she needs your help to stop the vampires" Green said

Lily turned around and faced Siena, she walked forward and embraced her like a long lost mother, tears drifted down her cheeks.

"I never wanted to hurt anyone, but I wanted to find you" Lily said "You left me here and I wanted to be with you"

"You mean after Jack and I went home?" Siena was also tearful "Why didn't you say?"

"I was afraid to ask, I just thought you would take me" Lily explained "I faced the vampires they wanted to turn me into one of them but decided against it as they needed the time portals to travel and thought they would stop this if they changed my body, altered my human structure in any way" She looked into Siena's eyes "I travelled through time searching for you opening new time portals, but never found you"

"So, why did you collect the dolls?" Siena asked

"They were for you, gifts from the ages" Lily explained "Some could talk, some had microphones in them, so real and unique"

"Thank you for your kindness to me" Siena hesitated "So what do we do to close the time portals?" She asked

"The secret is in the paintings, I discovered it when I tried to get to you, each painting contains a trigger that activates as soon as you touch the painting" Lily explained.

"Lily you can live with us, come with us and we can return home after we have sorted out the portals" Siena said

"You promise, do you definitely want me?" Lily asked

"Yes of course" Jack agreed

"Okay, let us return to the future" Siena said "To Darius castle"

"This way" Lily showed them the picture to travel through

"Wait!" Jack shouted "I will go first in case the slayers shoot you"

Jack was the first one to enter the picture, followed by Lily and Siena

They reached the castle and as anticipated the slayers were ready to fire on them, Jack dropped to the ground and shouted.

"Stop it's me"

Lily came next and Siena close behind, fortunately Carina was with the slayers and ordered them not to fire helping Jack to his feet. Lily was used to the time portals and walked out of it normally helping Siena up and then looking at all the slayers.

"This is Lily" Siena said introducing her friend

"So what do we do now?" Carina asked

"Lily will explain" Siena said looking at her

"Take away all the pictures from the walls, but leave that one" she pointed to one picture "That will be our passage to the twenty first century"

"Remove the pictures" Carina instructed

"Take tem outside and burn them" Lily said "Then we shall return to the twenty first century and repeat this"

"But, what shall we do about cubicles and changing rooms?" Siena asked

"They is only one end of the time portal that has a picture this is the port of entry, the other is controlled by this one" Lily explained

"Please join us for dinner" Carina said

"Okay" Jack said "We are in no hurry"

"Actually we are" Siena said "We need to get back home and plan our search for the vampires"

"Then you will need these" Gareth offered them a small device "This will pick up the vampires"

"This will pick up the green protective substance in their suits and help you track them down" Carina explained

Siena led the way through the existing portal

"Take away the picture when we leave" Lily said as they left

Lily was wearing a hat to hide her ears, she seemed happy to go with Siena and Jack, perhaps it was because she was entering a new life and had a family around her at last.

They arrived in a changing room in the middle of a busy store during a hectic shopping day for most people. Siena left the changing room first, the shop assistants looked at their odd outfits with a surprised look, unable to comment.

"None of your clothes fit us" Siena remarked

"I decided to go for the seventh century look" Lily said smiling

"I am with them" Jack said following them into the crowd.

They headed out of the store and into a busy street, looking around them

"Now where do we go?" Jack said bewildered

"Let's find out where we are" Siena said searching around with her eyes

"There" she pointed "A Birmingham bus going to Harborne"

"So we need to find a station to get home" Jack said

"Where do we go?" Lily asked

"Manchester" Jack replied

"Jack Clarke I hope you have money" Siena said

"Of course" Jack searched his pockets "My faithful flexible friend" he said showing them his visa card

They made their way back home to Manchester, arriving in Piccadilly station at night with people rushing around the platforms; suddenly Jack noticed a light flashing on his device.

"I am picking up a signal" Jack said "A vampire in the station somewhere"

"Walk forward down those steps" Siena said noticing a figure going swiftly down the stairs.

"The signal is getting stronger" Jack said walking down the stairs

Lily fell to the ground and appeared unconscious, a trickle of blood came down her nose, Siena attempted to wake her while Jack continued down the platform.

The area was dimly lit, as Jack continued down a platform hoping to catch sight of the vampire, suddenly a figure leapt out from the darkness, a man in armour with a green glowing light shining through it. Jack tried to fire his weapon but the vampire was right on top of him and knocked the weapon out of his hand, rendering him helpless. Jack wrestled with him but he was much stronger knocking Jack against a wall, Jack felt himself getting weaker but he was determined to beat this creature. Jack decided to fall limp onto the ground as if he was unconscious, the vampire exposed Jacks neck and showed his fangs ready to bite him, Jack reached out to where his gun had dropped and felt the handle. He managed to grip it enough to lift it up and aimed it at the vampire's chest, squeezing the trigger he managed to fire a bullet into him. The creature fell back with the impact and Jack shot him again in the chest and watched him disintegrate. Jack noticed another signal but it was fading, so he went back towards Siena and Lily, who by this time were both sat on a step.

"How are you Lily?" He asked

"I am alright just fainted sorry" she replied

"It's fine probably all the travelling" Jack said

But Siena looked oddly at Jack as if something was happening to Lily.

"I think we need to go home" Siena said

Jack never mentioned the other vampire as Siena seemed determined to get Lily home and get her to rest, Siena was concerned about her and felt that she would benefit from a good nights sleep.

Meanwhile in a warehouse in Manchester vampires were meeting together, Radius was leading them and appeared to be angry with them.

"Jack has found us, he has killed one of our vampires in a station" he said addressing his flock.

"But master he entered the time portal with Siena and Lily" a female vampire said

"Jessica, you should have stopped him" Radius replied

"But I had to warn you all" she replied "Besides he had powerful weapons from the future".

"We need Lily before she closes more time portals" Radius said "I want her alive" he insisted

"I am hungry" Jessica said dragging a woman from the corner of the room

"You are always hungry" He replied "Now go and find out where he lives"

Jessica bit into the woman's neck, then cast her aside, watching her drop to the ground, she spoke to Radius through a mouthful of blood.

"I will find Lily and return her to you master" Jessica said wiping the blood from her mouth.

"The vampire race will survive and my children we will feast off these humans and once more hail supreme over the nations, I tell you all this that our race will be the most feared in history. Fear the darkness for we are in the shadows and hungry for blood, our bodies yearn for human blood and we will take by force, go out and harvest the city my children.

HUNGER

Lily was the first to wake up in the morning, she walked into the bathroom and had a shower, she felt refreshed and ready to face the world until she looked in the mirror and noticed blood trickling down her nose. She was shocked at the sight of blood and began washing it away, at that moment Siena knocked on the door. Lily panicked and continued wiping away the blood, not wanting Siena or Jack to know, she thought they would send her home.

"Lily are you okay?" Siena asked concerned

"Yes I am fine I just got my period" she said making up an excuse.

"Do you need anything" Siena asked

"No, I have things thank you" Lily was aware of using sanitary towels from recent travels to the twenty first century "I am good thanks"

"Okay, anything you need is in the cupboard by the sink" Siena explained

Siena used to be able to smell blood as a vampire, she could tell when a woman was in her menstrual cycle which made them easy to detect in the dark, and they became easy prey.

Siena and Jack sat eating breakfast waiting for Lily to come out of the bathroom, finally she appeared and joined them at the table.

"Lily are you okay?" Siena asked

"I must admit I am still tired and I don't feel like going out today" Lily replied

"That's fine but you know we have to find the vampires?" Siena said

"Probably safer for you to remain here Lily" Jack advised

"Okay I will rest and join you later, maybe get a meal out" Lily said yawning.

Siena and Jack left the apartment later that morning and headed towards the city centre, in search of the vampires, little knowing that they were also looking for them. Jack traced his steps back to the platform where he confronted the vampire, before long he was picking up a signal which led onto a train, a armoured figure was rushing through the carriages occasionally looking back to make sure that he was being followed. The train stopped at a station and the vampire left the train and began walking towards a trading estate, once he reached a warehouse he walked inside and kept his armour on and suddenly turned to face Jack, the place stunk of rotting flesh.

"Well done Jack you have landed in my trap" the vampire said clapping

"Whose trap?" came another voice as Radius appeared in the shadows.

"Jack what a pleasant surprise" Jessica said "Delighted you could make it"

"I am fully armed and ready for you" Jack said holding an grenade

"Tut! Tut! Jack my friend you are slightly out numbered and are they the only toys that Carina gave you?" Radius asked

"Not exactly" Jack replied looking around the room

"Well believe it or not we only want Lily" Radius said "But we can destroy you and find her quite easily"

The warehouse was almost in darkness so Radius and Jessica removed their helmets, as they did so Jack threw a grenade at one of the vampire and shot his gun into the roof.

"Bad shot Jack, so disappointing" Radius ridiculed him

At that moment a series of explosions occurred and the roof caved in Radius and Jessica put their helmets back on and dived for cover, Jessica flew on top of some crates while Radius searched around the ground for Jack. Siena appeared on the roof and climbed down to Jessica throwing grenades at the other vampires and exposing their green suits, Jack shot at them causing them to disintegrate. Jessica began to fight Siena with other vampires each brandishing swords, while Jack attacked Radius determined to defeat him. Siena managed to knock Jessica off some boxes, causing her to stumble badly to the ground, Jack was also damaging Radius splitting his armour with his weapon and then attaching a grenade to his chest, and then jumping away from him. The grenade exploded crashing his armour and while he was exposed he shot him in the chest. Jessica escaped with two other vampires and headed for Jacks apartment, while Siena and Jack were being kept busy with the remaining vampires. Jack realised that they were heading for his apartment but they were faster than Him, Siena and Jack could only rush as fast as they could back to the apartment. Suddenly Jack had a thought.

"They are going to use the time portal in the art gallery" He said

"Let's go there and stop them" Siena said "We must be close to that one"

They raced to the gallery as fast as they could hoping to stop them, but just as they arrived Jessica stunned the security guard in the gallery and pulling Lily into the time portal via the picture that Siena came out of a few years ago, when she first met Jack.

Jessica took Lily through the time portal unaware that she was so ill, they arrived in the room Siena had originally escaped from, Lily had scratched her arm on Jessica's armour and the blood from her gash was dripping on the floor. They walked out of the corridor and found the main entrance to the castle, Jessica was still holding Lily by the arm and pulling at her, trying to hurry her up, daylight was approaching and although Jessica was in her protective suit she was afraid Siena and Jack would catch up with them and kill her.

"Come on Lily hurry" she said

"Stop please!" Lily shouted "I can't go on" Lily was holding her head in pain

Jessica noticed her nose bleeding and let go of her, she paused for a while

"You're sick" Jessica said realising how ill she was

"I am dying" Lily replied "How did you find me?"

"That broach you are wearing has a homing beacon we have been tracking you with it for years, ever since you were captured at Count Vermont's castle and we realised about the time portals". Jessica noticed Siena appearing from the time portal and flew away with the remaining vampires.

Siena rushed towards Lily while Jack raced forward shooting at Jessica, managed to hit one of the vampires but Jessica escaped. Lily fell to the ground holding her head in pain, Siena had followed her blood trail to the main door and realised her arm was injured, so seemed a little confused when she was holding her head.

Siena cradled Lily in her arms Lily began to cry, weeping silently against Siena's shoulder.

"I am sorry Siena" she said showing her the broach "They knew where I was because of this it has a homing beacon inside"

"What has happened to you?" Siena asked

"I became ill the last time we entered a time portal, I started bleeding I told you it was a menstrual cycle, so you wouldn't worry" she explained

"You need medical help Lily it could be temporal displacement, you could be seriously ill" Jack said concerned.

"No it's too late for me I know" she said shaking "I am so cold"

"But we can get you medical help back home, through the time portal" Jack said feeling helpless "We need to help you"

"It was the time portal that caused this I will never survive another trip" she explained "Please let me die" she said expressing pain with a grown and frowning "Please make the pain stop"

"I wish I could help you" Siena said with tears rolling down her cheeks

"I love you Siena" Lily said then looked at Jack "I love you too Jack" then she closed her eyes and passed away.

"Lily" Siena cried "I love you too Lily" She kissed her tenderly on the cheek "Don't die Lily please"

"Siena she is dead" Jack said touching her on the shoulder

"It's not fair, damn it" Siena said "Why did she have to die?"

"Siena we need to make plans" Jack said feeling tearful.

"No, I am not leaving Lily" she replied "I should never have left her"

"She was dying when we went hunting for the vampires, so don't blame yourself, that homing beacon told them where she was don't you see that?" Jack tried to explain "So what do we do now?"

At that moment Faith and Harmony appeared to take Lily's spirit away, they drifted down and took her with them back to the heavens. Both Siena and Jack looked astonished at this sight and remained silent for a while and then Siena looked at Jack.

"You go to Fargo and ask for his help, I am staying with Lily"

Jack never questioned her, but went as requested to seek Fargo in his usual place. After a short time Fargo hurried back with Jack and knelt beside Siena and Lily.

"I am so sorry Siena" Fargo said stroking Lily's ginger hair and toughing her right pointed ear "We have lost so much with Tom and Lily"

"I feel as if my heart has been ripped out" Siena said "We must rid this land of the existing vampires".

"Let us bury Lily first and then we will fight them" Fargo said "Take her to her home in the woods I will carry her home" Fargo said picking her up.

They travelled through the woods, to the cottage that Lily had lived as a child, she was buried beside a tree that Lily used to climb up looking over the meadow. Jack spoke a few words that were written by the lost poet John Gilbert Green and then they entered the cottage looking at the doll's that she had collected from various time zones. They left the cottage taking a few dolls with them and sleep over night at Fargo's cave dwelling, Siena looked back at the tree where Lily was buried and thought she saw Laura the witch standing over her grave. That evening they discussed strategies to attack the vampires.

"We need a plan" Jack said "We need help from the villagers in order to out number them and make sure no vampire escapes"

"The villagers will help, there are those who followed Tom" Fargo said confidently

"Great, so we will be well equipped and ready to fight as one army" Jack said excitedly

"No" Fargo said looking at Siena "They won't fight with her"

"Why not" Jack asked confused

"Because they still consider me a vampire, right" she said annoyed "Despite the fact I have killed countless vampires"

"They don't know that" Fargo said

"Well, can't you tell them?" Jack asked

"They won't believe it you must stay hidden, let us do the fighting" Fargo said

"Like that's going to happen" Siena said sarcastically

"He's right Siena you could get hurt and we don't want that" Jack said concerned.

"Sometimes I wish I had remained a vampire" Siena said angrily "The way humans treat me"

"We are concerned about you Siena" Fargo said trying to pat her on the back

"I am off to bed" she said shrugging him off "Alone" She said looking at Jack

Jack and Fargo remained by the fire discussing plan's of attack.

"Ignore Siena she is obviously upset about Lily" Jack said

"Yes, it is hard for her and I genuinely do like her, but the villagers would never understand or trust her" Fargo explained

Siena lay in bed clutching the broach that Lily once wore, her mind drifted back to happier times with Lily at the camp fire and the cottage. Then she thought about her dolls and travelling through time, the vampires and how they tracked her down everywhere. No wonder they could find their way to so many places harvesting the humans and feasting off their blood, she thought about what she said about being a vampire, but did she really want to live like that again besides she loved Jack and her life in the twenty first century did she really want to give all that up and live in hunger for the blood of humans?.

The next morning Jack and Fargo woke up, they had fallen asleep drinking wine and talking about many things, the fire had burnt down to a smoulder and both were snoring away. Jack awoke at the sound of Fargo yawning he jolted and opened his eyes widely, seeing the giants stretching and flexing his enormous muscles.

"Did you sleep well?" Fargo asked

"Not bad" Jack said scratching himself under the arms

"I wonder how Siena is today" Fargo said looking inside the cave

"I suppose I ought to wake the beast" Jack Said standing up

Jack walked towards the place where Siena had been sleeping but she was gone, he searched the cave but she was nowhere to be seen.

"Siena!" He called

There was no answer, she had gone during the night and somehow crept past the small ropes that would have tripped of an alarm namely tin cans tied to trees. She evidently was aware of them and avoided every trap, she could not have been abducted otherwise they would have been alerted by so much noise, and so Siena had decide to go.

A short while later Jack and Fargo went to the village and managed to gather a crowd together, they convinced a crowd of them to join in the fight to rid the land of vampires. Most of them were eager as they had experienced attacks in the night; some even spoke of green glowing demons snatching their children. One mentioned black vampires with white glowing fangs, some described them as six foot tall clad in armour.

Meanwhile at Count Vermont's castle Siena had been detected by Lily's broach and captured, it was as if she wanted to be caught, after all she knew the what the broach was used for and that the vampires would follow the signal and apprehend her. She was stripped of her weapons and armour and imprisoned in a room; she recognised the room as her own when she was in the castle with the other vampire women. The beige frilled curtains and four poster bed and oak furniture, she would now consider it as a dull room dark and un inviting, but then it was a wonderful place.

The door opened and Jessica entered the room walking gracefully in a black dress.

"Siena what a surprise" She said with Bramble creeping behind her

"Why have you brought that evil goblin with you?" Siena asked

"Be gone, creepy Goblin" Jessica ordered and walked closer to Siena

"You look so pale child" She observed

"And you are dark for a vampire" Siena said noticing her black skin

"Not all vampires are white my dear" she replied comparing her skin to Siena's

"So I gather" she replied

"You were once a vampire and now you're a human, how does that work?" Jessica asked

"I fell in love with a human" she replied

"Jack?" she asked

"Yes Jack" she replied

"So where is Jack now" Jessica asked "Have you fallen out child?"

"We have our differences" she replied reluctant to say much

"Do you miss being a vampire, living forever with your friends?" she asked

"Sometimes" Siena admitted

"Then let me help you" Jessica said "Come closer"

Siena walked towards her and Jessica began to stare into her eyes, she was trying to put Siena into a trance, making her feel out of control of her own body, and enticing her closer and closer until she was in her arms.

"That's good" Jessica said confident that she could control Siena "Now" she said gazing at the flesh on her neck "Let me kiss you"

Suddenly her fangs appeared and she proceeded to puncture her neck, Siena pulled away and felt blood trickling down her neck, she touched it with her fingers.

"No Jessica, I will never be a vampire again" she said looking around for an escape

"Don't be foolish child, listen to me" Jessica was angry "You could be a leader and fight the humans"

"No, I am human and I will fight you" she replied

"Fight me with what?" she shouted "You have no weapons"

"I have the greatest weapon of all" she replied "Gods love"

"So, where is your god now child?" she mocked her

At that moment a light appeared in the middle of the room and Jessica fled

"Faith" Siena said in relief

"I heard your prayers" Faith replied "Now be brave your friends are coming"

"Thank you Faith"

"Serenity is with them, now go and find your weapons and defeat this evil"

Siena went out of the open door and searched for her weapons, after a while she saw them on a table as if they had been placed there for her to find them. She grabbed the armour and put it on securing the traps and then grabbed her weapons and preceded towards the main hall, from the balcony she watched the slayers enter the hall from the door. Jessica ordered the attack and the vampires swooped down on them, the humans tried to break through their armour but found it impossible and so Jack began to throw grenades with Fargo and after half a dozen explosions weakened the vampires armour. Then Jack began shooting deadly bullets and one by one the vampires disintegrated, some of the humans used stakes killing more vampires until few remained.

Jessica attacked Siena they threw each other across the balcony, Bramble grabbed a speared and raced towards Jack trying to force it into him from behind but Fargo picked him up and with all his might dropped him onto his knee and snapped his back, his spine broke in two pieces and he lay helpless on the floor. Siena hit Jessica with her special blade splitting her armour and then Jessica managed to force Siena onto the ground ready to cut her throat, she brought the blade close to her neck and went to cut into it when a blast came from Jack's gun and she disintegrated. After this a human charged at Siena with a stake catching her side, Fargo picked the man up and tossed him over the balcony.

"She is a vampire" cried one human

"No She is human" Fargo shouted "See how the stake has merely scratched her"

"But she was once a vampire" another shouted

"No she is my sister" another voice was heard Catherine appeared out of the crowd and then went rushing up the stairs.

"She has fought vampires and proven to be worthy of forgiveness" Jack shouted

"Yes, my friends, we must thank her" Fargo said hugging her "And look she has a reflection in the mirror, isn't that proof enough"

"A vampire has no reflection" Jack said "Hold a cross to her forehead and she will not perish"

Catherine had reached the top of the stairs and held up a cross "See I have a cross" she held it to her head "And see I have garlic"

"She was forgiven by god and changed back into a human to fight these vampires" Jack said

"Catherine" Siena said "Thank god you are here with me"

"We have a lot to discuss my sister" Catherine said

Siena spent some time with Emma discussing the past, but although the villagers were told about Siena and her reformed character they still failed to trust her and considered that she would one day betray them and change back into a vampire. So Siena and Jack returned to the twenty first century leaving fond memories as well as bad memories behind them. Soon after their return Siena announced that she was pregnant and eight months and eight weeks later she gave birth to a baby girl she called Lily. Amazingly enough she had ginger hair but not I may add pointed ears.

As for the vampire there were reports of sightings in various cities, but what do you truly believe?....

PREVIOUS BOOKS BY SRS

30575712R00088

Printed in Great Britain
by Amazon